A DREAM OF
DEATH
AND
MAGIC

CHAOS OF ESTA ANDERSON
BOOK 1

SARINA LANGER

Interior Formatting by
PLATFORM HOUSE PUBLISHING

Cover Design by
DIABLERIE GRAPHICARTS

All books by this author

Relics of Ar'Zac
Rise of the Sparrows
Wardens of Archos
Blood of the Dragon
Shadow in Ar'Sanciond (#0.5)
The Relics of Ar'Zac Box Set

Darkened Light
Darkened Light
Brightened Shadows

Blood Wisp
Blood Wisp
Blood Song
Blood Vow

Find out more about Sarina's books at
sarinalanger.com

Content Warning

Please be aware that this book contains blood/gore, scenes and mentions of genocide, scenes and mentions of war, (perceived) animal cruelty/death (in nightmares only – no fictional animals were harmed in the making of this book), violence, death/dying, and torture.

Please also note that the slow-burn romance may eventually (in a book or two) turn spicy.

If these things are not for you, it's unlikely that you would enjoy this book/series.

To all of you who see the magic in the world.

To Miriam and Lady, my own Bonnie and, erm, Lady.

CHAPTER
ONE

A constant breeze whispers through my dreamscape. Before me and my spirit cat, Mischief, a meadow spreads as far as I can see. A crystal-clear lake glistens in the distance, and the grass is a lovely patchwork of red and green, because fuck realism. This is my dream and I can do whatever I want. I *have* done whatever I want, have seen every corner I know of in my thirty years.

But recently, I've had this niggle to go explore.

I lean against the black trunk of my purple-leafed tree, arms behind my head like a cushion, and breathe out slowly.

'Show me something new.'

Mischief, who loafs next to me like cats do, squints up at me. 'Not asking for much, then.'

I shrug. 'You can't honestly tell me that this is all there is.'

Dreams are awesome. They span our entire unconscious, so there's a *lot* of personal stuff to discover. Some of it is pretty dark and fucked up, to be honest—just like people. Most people don't think they dream at all because they don't remember it when they wake up, but we all dream. Most of us just don't *try* to remember.

And then there are some who enter their dreams, become conscious in them and take control, like I do. Anyone can do this, too, but most don't try because they either don't think they can since they, you know, don't dream *ever*, or because they think that lucid dreams are some kind of arcane bullshit. I don't really care what they believe, though. Their beliefs don't make my lucid dreams any less real.

I've done this since I was a child. The red-and-green grass stems from that time—my favourite colours back then. These days it's yellow.

I glance sideways at the tree trunk to think. Maybe it's time for a change.

I decide the grass is yellow from now on and watch it change. It starts where my feet meet the grass and spreads farther and wider from me until the whole valley is covered.

'I like it,' Mischief says. 'Looks even more like my toilet now.'

I sigh and shoot her a look. 'You're not spoiling yellow for me. It's the happiest colour and you won't change my mind.'

She slow-blinks at me, and I return the gesture to tell her that I love her, too. Mischief isn't a real cat—she's more like a fluffy bundle of shadowy sarcasm, a spirit guide or a dream guide—but I know more than enough about cats for her to behave like one... some of the time, anyway.

'So,' I say, 'about that something new? Where are we going?'

Mischief stands and stretches, front paws out in front and bum in the air. 'I don't know what we'll find, but—'

'There's something, I can feel it.'

2

'—but I feel it, too.' Mischief faces east, or what I know to be east with the unquestioning certainty of a dreamer. 'It's this way.'

I nod. 'I've been... feeling it for a few weeks.' I hesitate because *feeling* isn't quite accurate. It's hard to describe. It's like something is calling me, but there is no voice. It's more the knowledge that something lies that way somewhere, like very strong intuition. Like a new hobby you only just heard about but just know you have to try.

I can't wait to find out what it is. I haven't found anything new in my dreamscape for years.

'Shall we fly?' Mischief asks. 'Who knows how far away this is.'

I float into the air, spread my arms to both sides, and do a slow, savouring flip. I'm pretty sure I was a bird in another life. Being an Aquarius, air is my element, but this goes beyond star signs. I feel alive in a strong breeze. The first thing child-me did when she woke up in her dreams was fly, just to see if she could. I can conjure up whatever transportation I want or can invent, but I don't want anything fancy. I don't even give myself wings. I just take to the air and fly—anyone who's ever dreamed and flown knows you just *do* it. There's no science or real effort behind it.

Once in the air, my beautiful ginger fluff-bundle turns into a sparrow with soft-looking feathers. It's a smooth change, a poof in a burst of fog, probably because I love autumn and fog makes me happy. Even more so when there's a breeze. We've been in this damn heatwave for two weeks now and that's too bloody long. Bring back crunchy leaves and crisp air.

Besides flying, one of my first memories of lucid dreaming is seeing all this dreamscape for the first time. It's incredible how fast the landscape can change in a dream, or how strange it is. The for-now-yellow meadow lies below me; the glistening lake is ahead. Behind me lies a small village complete with a massive playground and a train station I haven't been to since I was eleven. My childhood lives there, but it's mostly empty now. I've grown up and moved on, and so have my dreams, although some smells linger, like my granddad's tobacco or my guinea pigs' hay. This song I loved when I was nine still plays in one of the streets; whenever I visit the town, it gets stuck in my head all over again. My parents' house sits just on the outskirts, but it's a strange fusion with the house I share with my sister and our dog now, my grandma's flat, and some garden I don't remember but that must have been important to me once. It's full of herbs, and I get the warm fuzzies whenever I enter.

That's just the stuff I can see at a glance. There's so much more behind those horizons.

And to my right—east—are craggy mountains with snowy peaks and deep ravines. No freezing-temperature snow though—I'm perma-cold, so there's none of that frost nonsense in my dreams.

Most of my fears live there, in the many caves and tunnels.

I'm no longer too sure about this. I've faced my fears—well, most of them—over the years and have come to terms with those I couldn't defeat. I do a lot of shadow work on the highest peak when I don't fancy the shadowy forest I created just for that. There are some things, though, I haven't been brave enough to tackle. I'm still terrified of spiders. I made the ones in my dreams talk because I figured they wouldn't be so bad then, but that backfired because real spiders don't talk. So I get on just fine with my chatty dream spiders, who let me know when they're nearby and just passing through, and I'm still scared of the ones in my walls and under my sofa. I'm fine as long as I don't think about it.

That I'm drawn towards the mountains now doesn't make me a happy kitten. By the look on Mischief's face, I'm guessing the feeling is mutual. She'd never abandon me or lead me into certain death—it's her job as my dream guide to, well, guide me, and no, if you die in a dream you don't die in real life—but it doesn't reassure me that she's unsettled by what lies ahead.

The air gets colder as we approach the mountains, and I let the breeze become stronger. It calms my nerves as we approach Terror Central.

As Mischief and I soar over the first peaks, I realise that the feeling tugging me onwards is still far away. Maybe it's not in the mountains after all, but… What's past the mountains? I've flown over them when I was younger and didn't reach the end, so I just assumed they had no end. Which was stupid of me, because Rule Number One of dreamscapes is *don't assume anything*. Everything can change so suddenly here that assuming you know anything for sure is stupid. Sometimes your unconscious needs you to understand that you can't control everything, even in a lucid dream or if you're a control freak. Nightmares still exist, although they're much rarer these days, and I try to confront them. Even so, I'm only human. I can get scared my mum's cough is more than a cold or that my moles have changed even though they're the same they've always been. I can still get paranoid that the guy walking behind me is following me. Fear is healthy, but as long as it exists, so do nightmares.

'What's this far east?' I ask Mischief.

She yawns.

Thanks.

'I don't know,' she says. 'That's the point, isn't it?'

In theory, Mischief knows more about my unconscious than I do. She's made of the same, or at least similar, stuff. If she does know more, she's not sharing, though—not because she doesn't want to, but because it would invalidate the journey. I still need to find answers myself. Besides, the unconscious landscape is vast, and if we assume that it covers past lives, every trauma we've ever endured, the entire collective unconscious... That's a lot of ground to cover, and I suspect that she doesn't have access to everything, either. Some secrets need to be stumbled upon.

'Let's go faster,' I say. 'I don't know how much longer I've got.'

Being in a lucid dream won't mean anything when my alarm goes off or my natural clock decides I've slept enough.

'Lead the way,' Mischief says.

I will myself faster. I wish it worked like this in real life, but I'm an atrocious runner and I hate jogging. Of course, if I could fly in real life, I wouldn't walk anywhere ever again.

After a good five minutes of speeding through the air, I add the Northern Lights for a bit of variety. Did I imagine the feeling? It's still there and I think it's getting stronger, but what if I'm just imagining it now because I think there should be a pull? What if it's just mountains after mountains after mountains?

Something glitters in the distance, like sun on a lake but black. My heart beats faster at the idea of an obsidian plain.

Come to me. Find me.

I probably imagined the voice, but damn if it didn't sound like me. Like I'm about to find a long-lost twin or a part of myself I never knew about.

I fly faster until I reach a lake so black, I can't see deeper than the surface. There are no waves or ripples, but something glitters here and there, like stars. It reminds me of the sky on a clear night, except there aren't enough stars to complete the picture and there's no moon. It feels a strange kind of empty, like it's about to pull me under and fill me with… with… I don't know. There's something beneath the surface, but I doubt I'd see it even if the surface were clear. It reminds me of that feeling you get when you're home late at night and suddenly feel watched. Knowing you're alone doesn't make the dread go away.

Whatever pulled me to the void lake's shores is waiting under the surface. I can't see anything, but I feel it watching me with a certainty I've never known—and yet I don't think it's a person or an animal or—

Mischief paws at my leg, and I stumble back. I've crept towards the lake without realising it. If Mischief hadn't stopped me, I'd be joining whatever's waiting beneath the surface. Deep down inside me, I know I wouldn't drown, but

I can't just shake a lifelong fear of deep water.

Now that I've moved backwards a bit, the pull is weaker. It's still there, but I'm in no danger of walking into the lake. That smooth obsidian surface is beautiful. Whatever is drawing me closer doesn't feel vicious or malevolent. It's just as curious about me as I am of it.

Part of me wants to jump in and completely submerge myself in the void-water, but I can't swim. If my unconscious decides that now is the right time to get over that fear… I'm not risking that.

But that doesn't mean I can't get closer.

'Watch my back?' I ask Mischief. I don't turn around to look at her. If anything jumps out of the lake, I won't let it catch me off guard.

'Esta—'

'It'll be fine.' I hope. 'Do you get any evilness from it?'

'No, but… There's something there. Be careful.'

I'm glad she's here with me. Mischief won't let me drown. The shock of going under would likely wake me up, anyway; therefore, there's really nothing to be worried about.

The closer I get to the water, the less I believe that there's something under the surface. It's not any one small thing that's watching me—the whole lake is waiting to see what I'll do next.

I swallow my fear and step right up to the shore. When I was a child, my parents loved going on holiday to warm places. I sat at the beach with my mum a lot. I couldn't swim then, either, but I still dipped my feet into the ocean. The worst thing that ever happened was when a small school of fish came up to my feet. My dad told me that, if I stood still, they'd nibble at my toes and it would tickle. I'm not scared of fish, but their number with the image my dad had put into my head freaked me out. I stayed on my beach towel the rest of the day. Somehow, I doubt there is anything as cute as little nibble fish in this lake.

I sit in front of the water and stare at it. Maybe, if I look long enough, I'll find answers in my dreamscape's biggest scrying mirror. I make a mental note to ask Kate, my neighbour, how to use one. Maybe that's the simple reason why this lake is here—my unconscious knows I briefly thought about scrying once, and this is its response.

That doesn't feel right, though. Closer, perhaps, but not quite there.

'What are you?' I ask the lake.

It doesn't answer.

I hold out my hand but let it hover over the surface. Part of me—most of me, actually—is still very unsure about touching it, and if I'm right and the whole lake is somehow one being... And I'm about to dip my hand into it...

I blink and shake my head. *It's a* lake, *Esta, calm the hell down.*

I decide to just get it over with already and lightly touch the void-water. It's... not wet, or anything at all like I expected. It's smooth, like satin. Tiny ripples move out from my fingers, but nowhere near enough to pretend that this is water. The refreshing feeling on my fingers doesn't fool me, either. It's more like putting your leg onto your cool duvet because you're too hot fully covered. A small smile spreads on my lips. I don't know what I've found or what I'm touching, but this feels right. Like it's been waiting for me all these years. Like part of me is whole now.

'You're leaning forwards, Esta.'

I jump back. That's twice now that I've nearly fallen in because I was too focussed on the pretty void before me. It may not be malevolent, but I'm not convinced it's all benevolent, either. So what if it feels like I've found a missing part of myself? Not every part of any one person is good. Even the nicest person has a dark side. What if diving into this lake would bring out the worst in me? All I did was touch my fingertips of one hand to it, and I still nearly fell into it.

'I think it's best if we sit over there.'

Mischief paws at my leg again. 'I think it's best if you wake up now.'

I want to stay and look at the lake some more, maybe try touching it again, but I realise how that sounds and decide that Mischief is right. While I'm this close to it, I'll be tempted.

'Promise to start far away from this tomorrow night?'

Mischief nods. 'Gladly.'

But she glances at it again, too. We're both drawn to it, and I know I'll be tempted to dive in during every dream from now on until I suck it up and do it.

When I wake up, my best friend and found sister Bonnie has already left for uni. Lady is resting her head on my bed with the world's saddest rottweiler-puppy eyes. I don't start work until one p.m., and since Bonnie starts her final year as a marine biology student in September, we've agreed that I'll walk our dog for now. Bonnie gets more studying done, and I get a bit of exercise.

I pretend to be asleep, but Lady doesn't fall for it. She whines, and I slowly open one eye. She lets out a happy bark and puts her paw on the duvet.

'What's that? You want a cuddle?'

She wants a walk, but I'll take every distraction I can get after last night's dream, and there aren't many distractions better than unconditional puppy love. Lady has been a puppy for the last seven years. We have a routine.

I pat the duvet, and she throws herself onto the bed. She lands on my chest so hard that it knocks the air out of me, but I can't help laughing when she gets comfy all over me, her head in the crook of my neck. Damn, I love this dog.

Bonnie and I adopted her when we moved in together. Lady was the runt of her litter—all the other puppies came running to us, tails wagging and eyes sparkling, but our puppy sleepily staggered around the corner and tripped over her own paws. Of course we fell in love with her. She's the only big dog Bonnie isn't scared of, partially because we raised her and partially because there's nothing scary about Lady. She's a cuddler, and we're both happy to oblige every chance we get.

I rub her back, and she nuzzles into me. When I put my other arm around her, we both sigh, and I'm pretty sure I've found heaven.

But it's nine a.m.—later than I'd like—so I cock my head and look into her eyes, which are pleading with me to not move. If she knew I need to get up so we can go for a walk, she'd be throwing herself off the bed and down the stairs, leash in her mouth and tail bashing into the door while I'm still falling out of bed.

'Come on.'

She whines again. I'd stay like this for all eternity, too, if I could. Our dog gets me.

'You mean you don't want to go for a walk?'

Her head shoots up, and she straightens.

'That's right. Let mama get up so we can get outside.'

She barks again and—yup, there it is. She throws herself down the stairs like the predictable pup she is.

I hurry in the bathroom and hate that I'm already sweating again two minutes after I leave the shower. Heatwaves are nice and all, but they weren't made for me and I wasn't made for them. Mum has often said how funny it is—apparently, I should be loving the heat since I'm cold all the time. If only it worked like that, but I'm terrible with both extremes. At least I can keep putting on more clothes when it's snowing and bury myself under a thick blanket with the heating on full if necessary. When you're too hot, you can only take off so many layers before you'd need to skin yourself, and I don't fancy that.

I put on the first dress I find—yellow, of course—and grab Lady's leash. Fortunately, my work place doesn't really care what we wear as long as we're decent, and it's the last day of my term-time-only shift before I get the summer off, so everyone is bound to be extra lenient. One of my colleagues wore slippers once, so I doubt my flowy summer dress will offend anyone. Not that there'll be anyone to offend—our little student-run gallery isn't very busy at this time of year. Everyone's gone home, so it's mostly myself and whoever else is working plus security. More staff than students.

I sigh, wondering if I should call in sick and crawl into the freezer, but my work ethic won't let me.

'Ready for your walk?'

Lady smiles at me. Half my family insists dogs don't smile, but what do they know? None of them are lucky enough to be owned by a dog or they'd know better.

The heat hits me the second I open the door, and I reconsider calling in fake-sick. Nothing and no one should have to put up with these temperatures.

'Morning, Esta.'

Lady barks her own good morning at Kate, my next-door neighbour, and her two dogs.

Kate laughs. 'And hello to you, beautiful.'

Lady runs over to the fence between our properties and jumps up so her front paws are on top. Kate scratches her ears, and Lady couldn't look happier. One of Kate's dogs mirrors Lady, and they sniff each other's faces like cats since there's a fence in their way.

'I was hoping to talk to you,' I say before Lady pulls me down the road. 'Can I ask you a few things about scrying?'

'Of course.' Kate places a kiss on Lady's head, and my dog looks downright in love. 'But perhaps later? I have some errands to run, and I think your dog is hoping to go somewhere, too.'

I smile at them both. They have such an easy friendship that I'm almost jealous, but all animals in this neighbourhood gravitate towards Kate. She says they tend to be drawn to witches, but I think it's more than that. They know she prefers animals to people—one of the reasons we became instant friends—and so they keep coming back. She knows the name of every cat and dog along this street, and she has the numbers of their owners just in case. I want to be more like Kate when I grow up.

'That would be great,' I say. 'I found something in—' I stop myself before I can mention the dream and the void lake. This isn't helping me forget about it. 'Doesn't matter. I'll talk to you later.'

We smile at each other, and I whistle. Lady comes flying. I fasten the leash to her collar, and off we go down the road.

Bonnie and I lucked out when we found this place. There are no houses immediately opposite us, just a park which is perfect for Lady. There are houses behind that, but they're far enough away that we don't get any of the noise. Most of our neighbours have either dogs or cats, so it was the ideal place to raise Lady. I can't go for one walk without meeting at least two other dogs. Naturally, the owners and I have never exchanged more than a polite nod and the occasional 'hi' or 'morning.' Our dogs know one another better than their humans do.

The air feels different this morning—cleaner, maybe, or more refreshing. A tiny breeze picks up and caresses my arms; it feels like a gentle air spirit has decided to greet me personally. It's *so* soft, a little like a blanket but without the fabric.

The guy who walks his two dogs twice every day enters the park from the other side—it's not a large park, more like a meadow—and our pups spot each other. My much bigger rottweiler reaches his Jack Russells in no time, and they bounce around one another like they've been apart for years. I've never seen two humans be this happy to see each other.

'Mornin', Esta.'

I tip my head. 'Morning.'

We briefly smile at each other before our attention is back on our dogs. Lady sniffs around his shoes and his two pups are jumping up my legs, so naturally the humans couldn't possibly talk. It's all about the dogs.

I'm glad he's never pushed me for his name. Seven years we've been doing this dance, and I've no idea what it is. I'm sure he's told me—we must have introduced ourselves since he knows *my* name—but I don't remember it. I'm generally bad with names.

His dogs are Sapph and Raff.

'Come on, Lady,' I say, worried she'll topple him over. He's an elderly gentleman and has walked on a cane for years; I'm always worried my dog's excitement is too much for him. He's never complained, though. In fact, he looks younger whenever he plays with Lady or talks to Sapph and Raff.

He chuckles. 'See you tonight, Esta.'

I laugh but shake my head. 'I'm not sure I'll brave the heat again, but it'll be Bonnie's turn, anyway.'

My best friend is a little fitness mad: one jog in the morning, karate every Monday night, and sometimes a second jog in the evening. Lady usually loves to join her for a run—she doesn't get that kind of exercise with me—but we all have limits. Bonnie's Spanish blood runs hot, so she does better with the heat, but Lady and I are happy to nope out of the sun and

15

back to the air con.

'How are her studies going?'

Bonnie must have told him. We're both socially awkward and have a hard time making excuses so we can just leave already, but he is a charmer. I admit we're both happy to talk to him… for the two minutes our dogs sniff each others' bums, anyway.

'Fine. She'll be done this time next year.'

I try not to dwell on it. She'll graduate in twelve months. Will this place still be big enough for her or will she get the hell out? Maybe she'll move closer to the sea. Lots of opportunity there. Eastgate isn't bad, but I can't imagine our river offers much to the future's best marine biologist.

'And will she stay here, do you think?' he asks.

I grit my teeth and smile through the internal pain. It's not his fault I'm internalising too much.

'I guess we'll see.' I give his dogs one last scratch behind the ears. 'Bye, Sapph and Raff!' They yap at me and wag their tails, happy to be spoken to. Raff puts his front paws on my knee—bless him, he doesn't reach any higher—so I pet his sweet little head again. I smile at my neighbour. 'Bye.'

One of these days, I'll have to learn his name, but today is not that day. I'm too awkward to admit that I don't remember it, so I make a mental note to ask Kate. She'll know. She probably has his number in case either dog wanders into her garden and falls asleep there. It's never happened with dogs, but with cats? She's prepared.

We say our goodbyes and Lady happily bounds across the meadow, inhaling a flower here and inspecting a blade of grass there. Tiffy's human enters the park with her, and the poodle and Lady have a good sniff of each other's behinds.

If only I were as good at making friends as my dog. She's so much braver, so much more social, than I'll ever be. I'll probably just become a hermit once Bonnie's living her best life in Brighton or some remote beach teeming with sea life she can discover.

But I won't dwell on it.

Only, the other thing I'd dwell on is the void lake, so I focus on Lady's beautiful curiosity and hope both thoughts will fuck right off.

CHAPTER
TWO

I admit, I sometimes hide at work. It's a small gallery, but they've crammed as many books into our basement as they could.

We're lucky to have our own library. There's more variety on the main campus, but why take the fifteen-minute walk across the park when we have so much right here? The shelves are packed with surrealism, psychology, a tiny bit of philosophy, cubism, sculpture, and all the art movements throughout time. We even have one book on Sumerian art. There isn't much spare room on the shelves, and I love them all the more for it. Most of our students don't refer to the books much—most prefer *doing* to *reading*, and when they do research, they use the internet—so it's become my space. I already found peace and quiet here when I was a student, and nothing has changed now that I'm working here. I've found a lot of inspiration in these pages, too.

But while I loved this place when I was a student and still love it now, I don't want to be here forever. Some of my colleagues have been here for over twenty years, and I don't want that to be me.

My eyes wander to the three surrealist photographs on the wall. My boss Eloise is the best for letting me exhibit them here. The gallery itself belongs to the students' work, and I'm fine with that—I had my chance when I was one of them. Now that I'm staff, I'm grateful that I can still show off my work at all, but it also bugs me that they're hidden away in the basement where no one important will ever see them. I want them to be shown in big galleries. I want recognition.

I'm also a coward and haven't approached anyone. My work needs something else, but I can't figure out what. Until I do, it's not worthy of those spaces. I want to put my best foot forward when I make my move, and my current portfolio isn't it. I don't know what *it* is, only that I haven't found it.

When Eloise offered to print my images and put them on the wall, I pictured every student stopping at my photos and admiring them, wondering who created them, being inspired by them. The reality looks very different. Most students barely spare them a second glance, and then it's likely more to wonder how they can get their work displayed in the same way. Not that they need it—they already have the gallery.

I sigh and look at the clock. One hour to go.

It's my last day before I start my summer break. Working term-time only has its perks; sitting here counting the seconds until I can go home reminds me of them during the quieter weeks. This job isn't perfect, but at least I won't be here when it's even quieter than this. We had eight students in today. Over the summer, there are days when we have only three. I'm glad I'll miss those days.

I should spend my time approaching galleries and creating new work, but there's been a block in my head lately. Approaching galleries is a whole different issue. I know my work isn't ready, so why should a curator care? The last thing I want is to make a bad first impression. These people remember you, and they talk. If I send a less-than-perfect portfolio out now, I'll never recover from it. There's a chance I'm overthinking it—Bonnie says I am—but I don't want to take the risk.

'What's this?' Eloise startles me when she walks around the shelf. 'Slacking off on duty?'

I smirk. 'Sorry. Are you struggling up there? Had a queue, did you?'

Eloise laughs and sits next to me. 'Security has just done a headcount.' A necessary evil so we know how many students are in the building. The space may not be large, but no one wants to lock up with someone hiding somewhere. Also, my managers are happy when they can show their managers how many students use which space when. 'Guess how many.'

'Well, we had eight earlier... Five?'

The few students who do come in now are on last-minute printing sprints before they take the next train home. There's always someone who waits to come in until five minutes before we close the doors.

'Two,' Eloise says. 'One was packing up, and I reminded the other one that we're closing. Security hopes they'll both be gone soon.'

I got super lucky with my boss. We have a very casual work relationship; but then, the whole place is pretty casual. If there are no students left by quarter to seven, security will kick us out early. They're also not above silently watching the last students from a corner until they leave. Usually, it doesn't take much convincing. We all want to go home, students included.

'Got any plans for the summer?' Eloise asks.

I glance at my photographs again. 'Make more of those. Maybe submit them to a few shows.'

'Good for you! They're wasted down here.'

Eloise is my biggest fan, right up there with Bonnie and Lady.

I shake my head, though. 'Not these. New ones. Better ones.'

She gives me that look. That don't-give-me-that-tone look. 'You're underestimating yourself. But if you can do even better, I want to see it.'

I smile, eternally grateful for her support and encouragement. 'You'll be the first.'

I mean it, too. Bonnie and Lady would likely see it a little before her since we live together and there's no one more easily impressed than my dog, but the first person I make a point of showing? It's always Eloise. And Kate. My parents are high up on that list, too, but they're too much like my dog: impressed by whatever I do and just happy to be included. I can't do wrong in Mum's eyes, and my dad doesn't know enough about art to push me. If this were something he did himself, he'd be pushing me all the time, but since it isn't, my art just gets his admiration. Or his confusion, depending on what I've created. They're not great for unbiased feedback, but on the plus side, I can always count on them when I need a boost.

'You should do it,' Eloise says.

I blink. Did I miss something she said while I was lost in thought?

'Do what?'

'Submit to galleries. You won't know if you don't try.'

I nod more to myself than in response. She's right, but it's not that simple. With the work I already have, it's not an option. I don't think it's bad, it's just nothing exciting.

You can't even jump into the void lake, Esta, and you know *you can't get hurt there.*

I hate it when my self-doubt is right. How can I expect to ever be brave enough when I can't even do *that?*

I sigh and look at my watch again. Eloise tells me about her summer plans—two weeks off to Greece in August—but I barely hear any of it. The memory of the lake is too distracting, but my hatred for my inaction is even worse. I should just do it. What's the worst that can go wrong? I mean, it's *my* dream, and Mischief is there to have my back. I'd be fine.

But I know my conviction won't last the walk home, so instead I discuss my favourite holidays with Eloise and thank the stars when security kicks us out twenty minutes early.

If there's one thing that relaxes me and helps me think or wind down, it's a walk in nature. My walk to and from work through our high street and along busy main roads isn't quite that, but I can still appreciate the breeze. Besides yoga, this is also the only exercise I'm prepared to do. On days like today, I'm grateful that I leave work so late; this heatwave would have been unbearable at four p.m. It's still hot now, but if I stick to the right side of the road, much of it lies in the shade from the buildings, and the breeze is picking up. I plug in my current favourite paranormal podcast and am grateful that, for the forty minutes it takes me to walk home, I won't think about the void lake.

Until just now, to appreciate that I'm not thinking about it. Damn it.

The high street isn't too busy at this time. The two local pubs have people sitting outside and some are waiting to be seated, but most other shops closed two or three hours ago. I consider buying ice cream, but then I remember all the ice lollies we have at home. I prefer something watery to something milky in this heat.

My eyes fall on the bookstore that opened about a week ago. Kate mentioned it to me and I've been meaning to go in, but I've been so focussed on getting home the last few nights that I forgot. Tonight, my eyes wander across the road. I'm surprised to see that it's still open. Kate said something about it having books about all kinds of psychological, philosophical, and paranormal topics, and many of the books in the window look old—yellowed-pages-and-vellichor old. Just my kind of place.

I quickly text Bonnie to let her know I'm stopping off on my way home so she doesn't wonder where I am, and head across the road. It takes a while because it's a busy road at the best of times, and it seems everyone is trying to get home right now. That, or they're trying to get their weekend shopping out of the way or go to a pub or the cinema or whatnot. I speed-walk across the moment I have an opening and pray the shop has air con.

It does. I couldn't be happier. That plus the smell of old books greeting me plus the look of old spines and paper and I'm in heaven. If they offer me tea, they'll have to accept that I'm moving in.

A little bell above the door announces my arrival. I'm the only one here, but I hear rustling from the back. A man who I'm guessing is in his late forties enters the shop floor and smiles at me.

'Welcome,' he says. 'Let me know if you need help finding anything.'

I return his warm smile. 'Thanks, will do.'

He stays behind the till, but since he's immersed in a book I don't feel like he's watching me or waiting for me to leave. I glance at my watch—it's 7:25 p.m. What if he's late closing the shop? I did think it's unusual for him to still be open, and I worry that I'm making him even later.

'What time do you close?'

'I meant to close at seven.' His smile tells me he doesn't mind. 'It'll be five from next week—opening week offer.'

I nod, sad that not more people are using it. Then again, he did mean to close half an hour ago.

'Sorry,' I say. 'I'll come back next week. I'll be on my summer break then, so I can come during the day.'

'Please, it's no trouble. Truth be told, it's been quieter than expected, so it's nice to see a customer.'

He winks, and I blush. Damn, now I have to buy something or I'll really be wasting his time.

'My neighbour said you have books on the paranormal, philosophy, things like that?'

Usually when I mention either to people, their eyes glaze over, but his shine a little brighter. He leaves the till and walks over to me.

'Just over here.' He leads me to a shelf along the left wall. 'Are you looking for anything specific?'

Well, there is that void lake… And I'm back here.

'Do you have anything about scrying or the collective unconscious?'

I'll already be talking to Kate about the former anyway; it can't hurt to do some reading before then, and my library has nothing on the latter. We have a couple of books on Jung, but nothing this specific. I suppose it isn't something our students would incorporate into their art.

I half expect him to give me a curious look—people always do when I mention it, so I've stopped—but he nods and pulls out two books. I'm not sure why I expected less, really—he does stock these, and he does want to make a sale. Their spines are a little cracked and the embossed writing has begun to fade, but they still look in good condition. He must look after them.

'Is this a passing curiosity or something you've looked into before?' he asks.

I wonder how honest I can be with him, but if I'm to come here for research more often, keeping the reason for said research to myself won't inspire trust. He'll also be able to help me better if he knows what I'm looking for.

So, I suck it up and say, 'I found a strange lake last night in a lucid dream. It reminded me of a scrying mirror, but I feel like there's more to it.'

He looks at me and gives me a slow nod. 'Well then.'

I'm not sure how to read the look he gives me—not judgemental, more like he didn't expect someone with those interests to walk into his shop tonight. When I scanned the shelves as I arrived, most did look to be more about general psychology. I glance towards where the shelf titles would usually be, but there aren't any. Another look tells me this is a small collection separate from the rest of the shop, certainly more specialized than the popular philosophy books I saw near the entrance. The books he handed me just now are more hidden away, like a secret.

I open the book about Jung's theory on the collective unconscious and find myself getting more into it than I have time for. I've read books by him before and adore his humour. If I'd been alive during his time, I feel we might have been friends or at least had a few interesting conversations.

'How much is this one?'

I get paid at midnight, and this book smells good.

Now he gives me a curious look after all, like he's waiting for my reaction. I brace myself.

'One-hundred and twenty pounds.'

I gaze at the book as I feel it slipping out of my reach. I'm happy to treat myself, especially where books like these are concerned, but I don't think I can justify that.

I nod and hand the book back to him.

'I'm afraid it's not meant to be.'

He chuckles. 'I might have a more recent paperback edition

in a box out back. If you can wait a moment, I'll have a look.'

I nod and browse while I wait. I like this little shop. Many of the books look like first editions, but I know they are more likely to be copies and later editions. Still, I shouldn't have startled at the price—these aren't books, they are treasure tomes.

One thing our city lacks is a good metaphysical shop. There are a few in nearby cities and towns, but I'm too lazy to hop on a train or a bus just for a short shopping trip. This shop has nowhere near the same stock variety, but it's better than nothing—so much better, actually. My eyes wander over titles like *Plato's Cave*, *The Egyptian Book of the Dead*, and *Herbal Magick*, and I already can't wait to come back another day. I guess this answers how I'll be spending my summer… if he doesn't mind me browsing more than buying. My eyes wander over some of the price tags, too, and I pray to every god who'll hear me that I haven't left fingerprints on any of them. If I ruin the quality of just one, it could ruin my bank account for a month.

He returns with a mass-produced paperback in hand. 'It's not as pretty, but it is ninety pounds cheaper.'

Still more than I hoped to spend on one book today, but it's easier to justify thirty pounds.

'Nowhere near as pretty.' I cast one last glance towards the shelf with the older edition. I already miss it. 'I'll have this one. Thank you for checking, especially because I kept you from closing.'

'No need to apologise—it's my fault for forgetting to lock the door. I'm glad I could help.'

'Want me to turn the sign over when I go?'

He looks at it and shakes his head. 'It's already the right way around. I'll just lock behind you.'

I turn around and gape at the sign. The Open side faces me, so the Closed side must be facing the road. How did I miss that? I shake my head at myself and hope my eyes convey how sorry I am.

'I get severe tunnel vision when I smell vellichor.'

He laughs. 'That's understandable.'

I smile and feel better about it. It's nice to use three-syllable words without being stared at—something that happens far too often with our students.

'Thanks,' I say again. 'I imagine I'll be back next week.'

'Remember, I'll close at five.'

I'd already turned around and made to move towards the door, but I look behind me now. 'What time do you open?'

'Nine a.m.'

I make a mental note, thank him again, and head home. Work was boring and I may be conflicted to all hells about the void lake, but I found a new favourite bookshop and I got a new book. The day didn't start great, but at least my summer break starts well.

CHAPTER
THREE

The moment I open our front door, Lady throws herself at me, tail beating against my leg and her face in mine. Bless her, you'd think she hasn't seen me in years. I hug her, inhale her doggy scent, and it starts to sink in that I'm off work for the summer. I can have this puppy love every day now, and I know Lady will adore it, too.

'Welcome home!' Bonnie shouts from the living room. 'Pizza?'

I'm pretty sure my lifelong BFF and I share a mind. 'Yes, please.'

I waddle into the living room so I can greet her properly, but it's hard to move when your dog, apparently starved for attention, moves between your legs.

I sit on the sofa next to Bonnie and immediately regret it. The cool leather really highlights how sweaty I am from my walk in this infernal heatwave. Everything clings to me. I didn't realise how wet my back is until I sat and leaned back into the leather.

Bonnie opens the website of our favourite pizza place on

her laptop and turns the screen so it faces me.

'What do you want?'

'Farmhouse, please. Tell them to murder it with cheese.'

I've no idea what Bonnie orders, because I hurry upstairs, fling my sweaty clothes into the laundry basket like they're poison, and turn the shower colder. I moan when the cold water hits my face, and for a moment, I simply stand under it as the water washes over me. I imagine I sit under a waterfall. I take a deep breath and let the water wash away the stress of the last academic year. While I'm at it, I also picture my lack of inspiration for my next project going down the drain. I've got roughly two-and-a-half months of me-time, but I know it'll go in an instant. I can't afford to waste my days on indecision. Maybe, if I can think of *just* the right thing and make it happen, *maybe* I'll approach our local gallery with it. But I don't know. That's a lot of maybes, and I haven't actually created anything yet.

At least now I have a new book to inspire me.

I smile as I think back to the book shop. I didn't even pay attention to the name, but I've a feeling I'll be spending a lot of time there over the coming months. So much inspiration in those pages, and it's all just waiting for me to discover it and make something beautiful. My heart jumps—I can't wait to see what I'll do this summer. It'll be epic, because I will make it epic. It's about time I took the next step.

The void lake pops into my head again, and I ask the water to *please* wash that away, too. That's a worry for a few hours from now, assuming the heatwave lets me sleep. Right now, I'm at the beginning of my summer break, pizza is on the way, and Bonnie has picked a movie for us to watch. We do know how to party.

I hold my face under the showerhead one last time and imagine the water as liquid gold. In my head, it's everything good—positivity, inspiration, joy. The water has washed away my stress, so now it's time to fill up on good things. Maybe it does nothing, but maybe it makes a difference.

I quickly dry off, which doesn't take long in this heat. I'm sweating again before I'm in my summer pjs. I saunter downstairs, because I've rushed enough over the last year; I've more than earned one calm evening. Of course, once I've created the project, I'll be busy with galleries approaching me and choosing which ones I want to work with, so this will totally be my last chance to relax.

I smirk at myself. I'll have to get a whole lot braver first.

I sit next to Bonnie. 'Thanks for ordering the pizza. How much do I owe you?'

She grins. 'Nothing. It's on me.'

I wave her off. 'You already bought last time.'

'Yes, but… I didn't have an internship with the Marine Biological Association's research aquariums then.'

I stare at her, and she giggles.

'That's amazing!' I'd hug her, but it's too hot and we both know it. Instead, we both laugh. I'm so proud of my sister. 'When do you start?'

'In two weeks, so we've got some time off together. I'll need to prepare, though, so it might be better if we do things in the evenings.'

The same as always, then. I can work with that. She has her

aquatic research stuff, and I have my photography. We'll make progress during the day, celebrate at night, and by the time the summer break is over, we'll both be better versions of ourselves. There, I knew I'd have a plan.

I get up and walk into the kitchen. 'Fancy a cocktail with the pizzas?'

She murmurs her agreement, and I get mixing. It's nothing special—gin, cranberry juice, and a ton of ice because it's too hot to risk these drinks warming up—but then I never claimed to be a mixologist. I've done this so often that my mind wanders for a few seconds. Bonnie is doing so well. Today, it's an apprenticeship, but tomorrow... Well, maybe not tomorrow, but there's zero doubt in my mind that she'll do incredible things sooner or later. Will I still be daydreaming about querying galleries when she's achieved her dreams, or will I have achieved mine alongside her? My mind wanders back to that lake yet again. It seems it and my goals are inseparable. I shake my head and will it away for later. Right now, we've got an evening to enjoy.

The pizzas arrive while I'm serving the drinks. We always order two large ones, because the leftovers save us cooking dinner the day after. Lady eyes the pizza boxes like they hold untold treasures.

We get comfy, and Bonnie starts the movie. I don't notice the title. The music is nice; it lets my mind drift. If I could dive into the lake... It wouldn't mean that I'd definitely be brave enough to chase my own exhibition, but I'm scared of both, and if I can't even do the easier thing...

I can't swim, though, so is it really easier? What's the real hurdle here?

'Esta?'

'Hm?'

Bonnie pauses the movie. 'Are you okay?'

I nod. 'Yes, sorry. There's this thing I've been thinking about all day. Hit Play, I'll be better.'

'It must be serious—you've barely touched your pizza. Want to talk about it?'

I do, but... Bonnie rarely remembers her dreams. She even used to insist that she didn't dream at all. Then again, if I can't even talk to my sister, who can I talk to?

'I found this lake in my dream last night.'

She sits straighter, which tells me she's taking this seriously.

'I felt like something was drawing me to it. When I got there, the pull was so strong I nearly fell in.'

'*Did* you go in?' She loves swimming—I imagine she was a fish in a former life.

I shake my head. 'I'd drown.'

'Even in your dream?'

'I... don't know.' Probably not. If I wanted to, I could probably just walk in and grow gills if necessary.

'Do you think it's important?' Bonnie asks.

I sit back and sigh. 'I think so? I haven't felt this drawn to anything in, well, possibly ever.'

'What's the worst that could happen?'

I stare at my pizza, hoping to find answers in the cooling cheese.

'How about this,' Bonnie says. 'Just jump in tonight, and I'll empty a bucket of water on you tomorrow morning if your alarm isn't enough to wake you.'

I smile. This is one of the reasons I love her—she doesn't get it, but she'll help. Mischief will be there, too. So, really, there's nothing to worry about, is there?

'Deal,' I say. 'But no need to drown me for real. Just poke me or something.'

We laugh, and she hits Play. My pizza tastes better after that, and instead of focussing on my fear, I focus on my imminent victory:

Tonight, I'll dive into the void lake, and tomorrow, I'll start a new photography project that *will* get me closer to achieving my goals.

CHAPTER
FOUR

I'm not quite as convinced anymore, standing at the void lake's shore and all. Mischief scratches her ear like cats do when a storm is approaching. I hope it's not symbolic for my impending doom.

She wasn't thrilled when I asked her to return here. It didn't take as long this time. I've been here once now—twice counting today—so I simply wished myself back, but we both remember the lake's pull. I thought I'd be scared the moment I saw it again, but instead, standing here feels right. I'm not unconvinced about having returned; I'm unconvinced about going for a dive. It's still tempting to simply walk in and grow gills, but my gut tells me that part of this is about trust. Trust the void lake. Become the void lake.

I smirk, too amused with myself.

'I'm glad you're in a good mood,' Mischief says. 'I'll remind you of that when I fish you out and punch the water out of your lungs.'

Apparently, all my uncertainty shows itself in her tonight.

'I don't think you'll need to.' I take a deep breath and dip my hand into the water. Like last time, it feels like satin sheets. 'I'm not sure what will happen, but I don't think I'll have to swim.'

When I take my hand out again, there's not one drop of water on my skin. It feels nice, actually, like I've used a good moisturiser. Something about this not being real water puts me at ease, too. I'm pretty sure I'd hate drowning, but drowning in soft fabric? How bad can that possibly be?

So, I dip my fingers in again and submerge myself to my elbow. It's so soft. Nothing grabs my arm from beneath the surface. Nothing even gently tickles my skin, the not-water aside.

I know with sudden dream-clarity that I'm meant to enter the lake. In some strange, inexplicable way, it feels like another part of me I never knew I had is calling me forwards.

'I'm going in.' I glance back at Mischief. 'Maybe get me out if I'm still there in ten minutes or so?'

Mischief nods, but we both know there's no need for a time limit. She is part of my unconscious, so if anything happens to me, she'll know.

Of course, that also means that whatever happens to me will likely take her out, too, but I choose not to think about that.

I feel weird stepping fully clothed into something that I thought of as a lake, but only until my shoes don't fill with water. For a moment, I stand immersed to my waist and look out over the surface. I no longer think of it as obsidian but as a fraction of the night sky during a dark moon. I let my gaze go soft, and it's like staring into the universe. My muscles relax.

My mind settles and expands like in a great meditation session. It's strange to feel seen by the void lake, but I do. I feel like the universe stares back, wondering what I'll do next.

So I take a step forwards, then another. I breathe through the slight panic when the surface reaches my chin. *It's not water. I won't drown. It'll be just like covering my face with a blanket.* I repeat it a few times like a mantra, and I still repeat it when I let my head go under. I force myself to keep my eyes open to reinforce my point that I won't drown.

I can't tell where the surface ends and the inside begins. It's all darkness and distant stars sparkling in the thousands, probably millions. They call me forwards, so I start walking. Only my legs don't move. I'm floating. When I look down, I no longer have legs or feet at all, or a body. I've become a being of pure energy, or perhaps a thought. Honestly, I don't know what to call it, but I *feel* whole.

Something inside me changes, expands. There's a comfort to it, and I realise this isn't some other part of me at all. I didn't misplace anything, I just forgot I had this muscle or sense or whatever this is. Like I've seen the world without yellow this whole time—a tragic thought, I know—and now my sight is complete.

Mischief is no longer waiting for me by the shore. All of me is needed for this, and that includes my little dream guide.

I float perfectly relaxed and at peace for an eternity or two, knowing that I've opened myself to something I can't comprehend yet. I don't try to wake up. I don't try to leave the lake.

And when my alarm wakes me up, I need a moment to

remember that I still have a body, that it was just a dream.

My morning is disappointingly normal. I don't know what I expected, but I thought something would be different. I thought maybe I'd be filled with ideas, too many to work on right away so I'd need to write them all into my notebook and be grateful for the divine inspiration. Instead, it's a morning like any other.

Bonnie gives me a curious look when I enter the kitchen to pour myself cereal. When I woke up, she was just peeking into my room to check on me.

'And?' she asks. 'Did you?'

After our discussion last night, there's nothing else she could mean.

I nod. 'It was neat, I guess? I don't know. I expected more.'

I didn't think I'd be this disappointed, but then I didn't think that nothing would have changed.

I cock my head and look down myself. 'I haven't grown another hand or anything, have I? My skin is still deathly pale? My eyes are still grey?'

She walks over and gets so close she nearly touches my nose with hers. 'Yup. Sorry. No galaxies in there or anything.'

I sigh and grab the cereal box. I pour the milk into a mug and heat it in the microwave. Bonnie thinks I'm a monster for having hot milk with cereal, but it tastes so much better even in a heatwave. Some standards you just don't compromise.

Bonnie puts her plate by the sink. 'Leave it, I'll wash up later. I'll go walk Lady first.'

I nod again, but then I change my mind. 'Do you mind if I

take her? I wouldn't mind a walk.'

There's nothing better for clearing my head. Maybe it'll help with disappointment, too.

She shrugs. 'No, that's fine. I was hoping to go swimming, so now I can stay longer.' She winks at me and runs upstairs, I'm guessing to pack a towel and bikini.

Lady whines at me from the door.

'Sorry, baby, we haven't forgotten. Do you want a tea while you wait?'

She barks and comes running. The water is still hot from Bonnie's coffee and my tea, and there's enough left for one more cup. My dog is picky with her tea—she'll lap it up when Bonnie and I make it, but when my parents come to visit and make her a cup, she doesn't touch it. Our puppy knows what she likes.

She slobbers her tea while I finish my cereal and my own cup. I'm not normally a fan of cereal milk and tea, but after last night's gigantic let-down, I'm all for comforting caffeine. As soon as we're done, she runs to get her leash. We have it on a hook on the wall, but she's figured out how to jump up and get it down. She sits and waits with that begging stare while I put on my shoes.

'Come on, then,' I say to her, and fasten the leash to her collar.

Bonnie and I shout our goodbyes and have-a-good-mornings up and down the stairs, and then I'm off.

The heat assaults me instantly. It's odd—I don't remember moving to the surface of the sun, but here we are. Lady, at least, doesn't care. She's just happy to be outside and going for a walk with me. It probably helps that her hair is short. Me, I had to learn how to tie a high bun. My hair is too long for heatwaves and stuck to my neck in sweaty strands until I learned what a hair doughnut is and how to use one.

No sign of Kate this morning, so Lady and I head straight to the park. I woke up a little later today, so I probably missed her. Come to think of it, though, I feel refreshed. Last night's dream was disappointing beyond belief, but I guess I got a good night's sleep out of floating around the universe.

We enter the park, and I let Lady off the leash. She throws herself into the grass like a majestic meadow dolphin. I whistle and stroll towards the other end. Sapph and Raff run towards us before I even see their human. They jump up my legs to say hello, and I scratch their ears. They don't stay long—they like me, but they love Lady. When I spot their human, our eyes meet and I wave. I squint against the sun. Something seems different about him, but I can't put my finger on it. Like his beard is fuller, only… He never had a beard, did he? How did he grow that over night? Why would he keep it in this heat? The things people do for fashion, I don't understand them. And in his defence, it's not a full-on bushy beard, more like thick stubble. There's probably a name for it, but fashion of any kind and I don't go together.

'Good morning, Esta.'

I smile and wave. 'Good morning.'

Damn it, I meant to ask Kate what his name is. Feeling awkward and like he must know that I've no idea, I nod to his stubble.

'It suits you.'

'Hm?' He touches his stubble with one hand and gives me a surprised look. 'Do you mean this?'

I nod. 'I didn't know you could grow a beard so fast. Or, actually, my dad has to keep his trimmed because it grows back so quickly. I guess yours does the same thing.'

Please don't ask me why I never use your name.

He gives me a strange look, like he's not sure what to make of me, but his eyes soon soften and his smile returns. 'Thank you. Barely anyone ever notices.'

I laugh nervously. 'Yeah, people are like that, aren't they? That's why I always tell myself that it doesn't matter if I'm not happy with my hair. No one but me will notice!'

He nods like it's the same thing. 'Sapph. Raff.'

His dogs stop playing with Lady, stare at him for a second, and run over to us.

'I'm afraid I don't have much time this morning,' he says. 'When you get to my age, it's one doctor's appointment after the next.'

I nod like I absolutely know the problem.

'Nothing serious, I hope?'

'No, just the regular.'

'Good to see you,' I say before he can use my name again. Him saying it first makes my ignorance worse, like it's rude to not use his when he made the effort.

Lady longingly looks after his dogs as they leave the park, but she quickly gets over it when she spots a family around the playground equipment. I call her back when she does a quick walk towards them.

'They don't know you, baby. They might not like you

jumping all over their children.'

She looks at me and whines.

'I know. Hard to imagine how anyone wouldn't like to cuddle you, isn't it?'

I pet her head, and she barks in approval. She loves children, though—well, she loves meeting new people no matter their age—so we saunter in the general direction of the playground. The air shimmers from the heat around the family Lady was interested in—one boy, one girl, and two women who I'm guessing are the mothers. I'm guesstimating the kids' ages to be around ten and five, but to be honest, I've no idea how old children are. They all look five years old to me until they're suddenly teenagers, and then they look roughly sixteen until they're grown-ups. I know my parents are disappointed that I've no intention of having children, but they'll just have to deal with it. They don't like it, but they're slowly accepting that Lady will be their only grandchild unless we adopt another pet.

I blink at that strange shimmer around the family. *Is* it the heat? There are other children and grown-ups around, and none of them have this glimmer. It reminds me of a mirage, but we're nowhere near a desert. It has been hot enough here that the road shimmered like this, like it's wet even though we haven't seen rain in weeks. The grass is barely grass at this point.

Although, when I've seen the wet-road illusion, it's always been a line. What I'm seeing now is happening *around* one family; it doesn't cling to them or anyone else. It almost looks like...

Wings.

I check my bag and sigh at my stupidity. I should have brought water. It's dangerous to get dehydrated in this weather.

Lady puts her paws on the fence and watches the kids play on the swings. When they're in the air, they hover for a moment too long, like they're the ones flying and the seat is just along for the ride. I focus on my dog before I get dizzy from all these mirages. This heatwave has got to be breaking some records.

'Come on down,' I tell her. 'You don't know these people. They might not like dogs ogling their children.'

She whines again. One of the mums comes over. She dons a patient, loving smile for my dog, and I immediately like her. Dog people are good people, at least most of the time and definitely in this neighbourhood.

'Sorry,' I say. The mirage-shimmer-thing is still there and moving with her, like there are actual wings coming out of her back. I try not to stare at it, but damn, I want to stare at it. That's not how I was raised though. Besides, it's definitely the heat. It's the only explanation that makes sense. 'She gets carried away when she smells new people.'

The woman laughs. 'That's alright. Dogs tend to greet us, so we're used to it.' She nods to her children. 'They're a little young for it, though.' She leans in and whispers, 'My wife and I have talked about getting a dog in a year or so, but don't tell them that. They'd be insufferable.'

I chuckle and nod. Since I haven't seen them around much before, I'm guessing I only ran into them today because it's

43

the weekend, when Bonnie would usually walk Lady, and because I overslept a little. Keeping their secret should be easy.

'Thanks for understanding,' I say.

Not everyone likes being assaulted by my overly friendly dog. In other parks and along roads, we keep her on the leash, but all the pet owners around here know each other. We're all good with one another and our pets.

I give my dog a hug. 'Let's go home. Mama needs water.'

Because I swear I can still see wings, and only on this family. Like the heat is more concentrated around them or… something. The woman nods and walks back to her wife and kids. The wings move with her. Maybe I didn't sleep as well as I thought. Maybe it really is a special kind of mirage. Or maybe…

Maybe I'm really just very dehydrated.

Ever since I was a child, I've been hoping for there to be more to this world than we can see. As a grown-up, I'd also like to think of myself as rational. If fairies existed, someone would have noticed. Although a fairy couple taking their young fairy children to the park like any other family sounds like an interesting idea, and an interesting photography project. Not that I know how I'd photograph it, but maybe…

I shake my head—carefully, so I don't get dizzy—and start the walk home so I can drink a litre of water.

Lady gives me a sad look when we're back home so soon, but I don't want to start my summer break with a heat-induced migraine. Now that I'm home and pouring a big glass of lemonade, I don't feel that bad. I actually feel pretty good. I want to move more, explore more, not sit down and wait to feel better. Not when I'm already feeling this good. I've been out in the heat too long before, and it was nothing like this. Once, when I was younger, my parents took me on holiday somewhere local. We went for a walk through this town on one of the hottest days of the year, and I didn't wear a hat or drink enough. We'd been out in the sun for about two hours when the heat got to me. I thought I'd throw up. My head was splitting in two. Everything was spinning. That's what I expected to happen today when I saw those wings, but so far... nothing.

So maybe it wasn't a heat stroke. But if it wasn't that...

No, my mind had to be playing tricks on me. Wanting supernatural beings to exist and actually seeing one—or a whole family, in this case—are two very different things. Someone would have noticed by now. There'd either have been unavoidable news on every TV channel and pop-ups on every website, or we'd be so used to it that I wouldn't be scratching my head now. So what did I see, if it's neither that nor a heat stroke?

I take my lemonade outside and sit in my favourite shady spot. Near the back of the garden, there's this massive tree— I don't know what kind—with low-hanging branches. On a breezy day, the leaves rustle and the wind strokes my skin. Bonnie and I talked about having a wooden platform built, maybe some nice outdoor furniture, but I don't really need any of that. Just sitting here on the mercifully cold concrete of some long-gone shed or summer house and under the shade of the tree is perfect for me. Even more so when the breeze picks up a little as if to greet me.

I close my eyes and turn my face to it. 'Hey, breeze.'

I sigh and let my mind go blank for a second. I run my hand over the concrete. It would look a lot nicer with some decking, but wood doesn't stay as cool as concrete. I've seen cats lie under this tree in hot weather. Bonnie and I have been saying every heatwave since we moved in that it would be terribly unfair to rob them of this cool oasis, but really we're just too lazy to find a company to deal with it. That, and there are other things we prefer to spend money on. Like celebration pizza. Or consolation pizza.

Something about the fairy family tugs at my memory. It would make a great photography project, since not many photographers have a supernatural portfolio, but wasn't there someone… I don't remember the name, but I'm sure I came across one photographer who had a whole series of fairy images. Nothing as clear as what I saw today, but then I don't know how their wings would come out on film or digitally, and frankly they weren't that clear in the playground, either. I also didn't want to be rude and stare at them. I could kick myself for not remembering the photographer's name, but I didn't think it would be important. I didn't study those images since they weren't relevant to my research at the time. For all my wishing that fairies, vampires, and whatnot exist, those photos didn't look real to me. I figured the photographer or an assistant had introduced a trick of the light or something to make them appear real. And weren't they proven fakes anyway?

But my gut won't let it go. There's a small voice in the back of my head that whispers, *If you're so determined not to believe it, how will you ever know it when you see it?*

Some days, that voice sounds a lot like Mischief.

I've had so many chats with Kate about the importance of being open-minded, but here I am, searching for some other explanation.

If I went back to the park right now, would the family still be there? Would I see wings again, or would my mind not be able to trick me twice?

I gulp down the rest of my lemonade and go to get Lady, but she's fallen asleep on my bed. Bless her. She would want to go out again if I offered, but she looks so peaceful that I don't want to wake her.

I leave a note for Bonnie on the kitchen table, letting her know that I've gone for a walk, and head out. The easy thing to do would be to ask Kate if she knows anything, but I don't want to overreact. If I see more fairies, I'll go ask Kate. If I don't see anything else unusual, I'll drop it and blame the heat.

I let my mind wander as I stroll back to the park. I don't want to explain away something real, but I also don't want to read too much into what I saw.

Kate once told me that magic is just science that hasn't been explored yet. If you want to know if a spell works, it's no good to assume that it won't; you try it and record the results. If you want to know if you have an aptitude for tarot, wondering won't get you anywhere; you buy a deck and do a few readings.

So, I head straight to the playground. If the family is still there and I didn't imagine the wings, I'll see them again.

I'm sad when I reach the playground and the family is gone, but my disappointment doesn't last. More people are around now. My heart begins to race. I should have brought my photography notebook, but something tells me I won't forget any of this.

There's a small rise overlooking the meadow, so I sit on the grass and observe in awe. My brain is still trying to make excuses; I note them and move on.

Two girls play football on the small court. Black tails hang out from under their shirts.

A family—two men and a little boy—have a picnic not far from me. Fluffy white wings stick out from their backs.

A man and a woman walk their Labrador. I don't see anything different about him, but she has wings similar to the fairy family.

I must be missing a ton of detail, but I don't want to stare at any of them too long. Other people are around, too, but I don't notice anything out of the ordinary about them. They're either hiding it well or they're regular humans, like myself.

I lean back into the grass and watch the clouds. My lips curl into a stupefied smile. I suppose they're all hiding it or this would be bigger news. Surely I'm not the last person on earth to catch on? I don't remember a lifetime's worth of conversations that made no sense at the time. Every time anyone talked about werewolves, vampires, or anything else supernatural, it was about a movie or a book.

Why am I seeing all this now? The void lake comes to mind. It's the only thing I can think of since I haven't done anything else differently or new. I wouldn't have felt so drawn to it if it weren't important, but that doesn't explain how no one else is seeing this.

My heart races as I stare into the clouds. It's starting to sink in that I'm surrounded by all kinds of beings I never realised existed, and my confusion is turning to... well, not panic, but not joy, either. Are those children with the tails demons? They don't look evil, at least no more evil than other kids. They're playing football like non-demonic children. The only thing they're hurting is their parents' bank accounts. The fairies don't seem to be up to any evil mischief, and the lady I talked to earlier sounded lovely. If those men are angels, I suppose they can't be evil.

Unless it's all lies.

Unless it's all true.

I sigh and take a deep breath in. Worrying about it won't change that they've been around me this whole time. It's not their fault I didn't notice until today.

I jump upright with a gasp when something bumps into me, but it's just the football. One of the maybe-demon kids runs over but stops a few metres away from me, eyes big and pouting. Who knew demons were so concerned about stranger danger?

I roll the ball back. 'Here you go.'

The girl giggles. 'Thank you, miss.'

Damn, she's polite. More so than most of the students I talk to at work. Maybe she's not a demon after all.

Or maybe I've no idea what demons are actually like. It's not like I've ever met one.

Unless I have and just didn't realise, which seems likely as of today.

I glance at my phone. I've been here for half an hour, so it's still early. Did I ask that bookshop guy if he opens at the weekends? I could consult the internet, but I've a feeling that any search of *are demons real* won't result in anything useful. The bookshop seems more likely, and if I'm lucky the owner can help me find relevant books. That, or he'll give me funny looks when I ask, but I don't think he will. He seemed positively surprised when I asked for books on the collective unconscious before. That's not quite the same as angels, demons, and fairies, but I did see some books on the paranormal, so hopefully he won't kick me out when I ask. It would also be a terrible business strategy, so he probably won't.

I get up and drink half my bottle of water. Mum always said I don't drink enough, but heatwaves make it easier to remember.

Before I head to the high street, I stop off at home, put another bottle of water into my bag, and take Lady with me. She's bouncing all around my feet and hitting my knees with her tail, happy to be going for another walk so soon. I owe her a longer adventure, and since she's awake now, I might as well.

As we walk, I remind myself not to stare at people. Lady would let me know if any of them are bad guys; she's got a great people radar. That she embraces most of the strangers we meet on our walks reinforces my idea that nothing has changed, at least not with them. My perception is different, but everything else has stayed the same.

Still, it's really hard not to gawk at some of them. There are so many people with different kinds of wings, I almost feel left out—why did I have to be a boring, regular human when there's so much variety? Is one born a fairy, werewolf, vampire, angel—or can one become one? The wings alone come in all shapes and sizes: feathery angel wings in white and black; shimmery fairy wings, which come in yet more shapes and all colour combinations; leathery wings, which I'm assuming are demonic. Some of the latter also have tails, others have scales, and yet others have tails but no wings.

If the bookshop has anything on this at all, I might be reading through those books for the rest of my life.

A couple spots me staring from across the road, and I quickly look away. To avoid drawing more attention to myself, I focus on my dog. Lady seems as happy as always, entirely unaffected by my new super-vision. Does she see what I see? Have dogs always been able to? What about other animals?

So. Many. Questions.

I doubt I'll find a handy encyclopaedia, but I'd appreciate the hell out of one. My mind wanders to one I saw a while ago. What if none of the entries are fiction? Maybe I should start there after all.

We reach the bookshop too quickly. There was a lot to take in on the way, and I don't notice much else once I'm lost in thought. One look at my watch, though, tells me I took nearly fifteen minutes longer to walk this far. I blame the miscalculation on the heat and the supernatural distractions.

I tie Lady's leash to a bike rack in the shade and make a mental note to ask the owner if I can bring her inside next time. Most shops don't allow dogs, though, so there's nothing

I can do about it.

I sigh when I enter the shop and the air con hits me. We need one of these at home, but heatwaves like this don't last long enough and aren't common enough for shops to sell them cheaply.

The owner smiles at me from behind the till. He's reading again, though it's a different cover. It's nice to see a bookshop run by a bookworm—makes it cosier and more authentic somehow. Maybe he's hiring? It probably wouldn't pay as much as my gallery job, but it wouldn't be as annoying, either, and it's closer to home. Plus, the staff perks are better—one glance at the shelves says as much. But since I'm the only customer here again, I doubt he can afford to pay me. It's sad, but I'll be lucky if this shop survives its first year.

'Back so soon?' he says.

I return his smile. 'I thought of some research I can do.'

He stands and walks over. 'Can I help you find anything?'

I swallow and pray to the stars that he won't find it weird. 'Do you have anything on paranormal sightings, experiences, hauntings, that sort of thing?'

I brace myself for the usual odd look, but he nods and heads to a shelf on the right. Grateful and excited, I follow him.

He points to the whole wall. 'There's quite a lot, most of it old. Much of it leans on various mythologies and dates back rather far, but I think you'll find something you like.'

I smile all my gratitude at him. 'Thank you, I'll look through them.'

Why can't my gallery have these? Oh, right, because it's not relevant to the vast majority of our art students.

I let my eyes roam over the shelves. Some of the books look like they're originals in languages I can't read, but I'm hoping that's just the covers. Even if I really can't read them, there are plenty of other books here. I can't wait to pick one and start, but how am I supposed to choose? I want all of them.

Every now and again, we see a student who maxes out their borrowing allowance, and we always shake our heads at them—they can't possibly read all twenty books at the same time; they'd be better off taking one or two, working their way through those, and then coming back if they need more. Standing in front of these shelves, I feel their indecision. There are a lot more than twenty books here, and I'd take all of them if I could. Even the ones I can't read, just to inhale their scent.

'You're not hiring, are you?'

He laughs. 'I'm afraid not, but you'll be the first to hear if that changes.'

There's a twinkle in his eyes, and I laugh. I knew the idea was too good to be true.

'Let me know if I can help with anything else,' he says.

I nod. 'Will do.' I glance towards the till, where the book is waiting for him. I smile at him and nod towards it. 'Happy reading.'

He smiles back and gets comfy on a stool behind the till.

I return to the shelves and run my hand over the spines. Some of these must be ancient. I'm scared my touch will crumble them and then I'll owe him thousands of pounds, but if they were that fragile they wouldn't be out here where any parent can bring in a spoiled kid to run their sticky ice-cream fingers over the books. They'd be in a safe somewhere.

I pull out a book at random—the fabric cover pale and torn in places, the writing too faded to read—and open it. The beautiful scent of old books hits me, and I sigh again. Gods, I want to live here. Maybe the owner will be my friend, but for that to happen I'd need to ask his name, and me and names... Besides, it's weird to ask an employee for their name. In my head, only people who are about to complain to the manager do that, and I have zero complaints about this place. The few rare times visitors to my gallery have asked for my name made me feel uncomfortable—none of them complained, they were just nosy—and since it's on my name tag, I didn't really have a good reason not to answer. Still, it feels weirdly private, despite it being written on my staff badge. This guy seems nice; I don't want to make him uncomfortable. Even less so because I have every intention of spending at least half my summer here.

I take another deep breath with my nose in the book and put it back. One glance at the page tells me I can't read it, so there's no point leafing through it; although, what if there are illustrations? I make a fist and bite my lip—no, bad Esta! You'll never leave if you get distracted by pretty pictures!

I pull out three that sound promising—*The Super-Natural in Ancient History*; *Living Among Us—Stories of the Paranormal*; and an actual encyclopaedia. The latter is massive and weighs too much to carry, especially in these temperatures, but the walk home will be over so fast. Once it's mine, it's mine for life. Totally worth twenty minutes of pain.

I just hope he has a bag. I did bring one, but it's not big enough for these three, especially the encyclopaedia. My water bottle already takes up most of the space. I could have prepared better, but I didn't think I'd find such a monster of a book.

I heave them to the counter and worry I've broken the surface when they drop onto it. He gives me an amused smile.

'Will you need a bag?'

I sigh in relief. 'Yes, please.' Just carrying them over here was rough on my weak arms. If he hadn't offered, I'm pretty sure I'd have left the encyclopaedia for another day.

'Interesting choices,' he says. '*Good* choices. Pardon my curiosity, but may I ask what draws you to this topic?'

I hesitate. People can be judgemental, especially where the supernatural is concerned. I was much more open about it when I was younger, but you only get that look so many times before you stop—that look that says *I didn't know she was such an airhead.* I'm done with it. I just want to read and learn in peace.

But I don't think he would judge me in the same way. It's his book shop after all, and I don't believe for one second that he only stocks these because they're bestsellers.

'I'm sorry, I shouldn't pry,' he says. I guess I hesitated too long. 'Most people who come here turn their nose up at this section.'

I smirk and glance around the empty shop. 'Most people?'

'Before I moved here. The shop was a little busier, but not much.'

I nod. 'It's personal interest.' My heart hammers. Normally I'm only this honest with Bonnie and Kate, but I feel I can trust him. And he did ask nicely. 'I… I'd like to believe that there's more to the world than we can see. I don't know about vampires and fairies and all that, but just *more*, you know?' I'm aware that I'm rambling and stop myself. Since this morning, I do know about vampires and fairies and all that—or about fairies, anyway—but I still worry he'll think me a childish idiot who has her head in the clouds rather than in reality. Besides, even if he didn't, it's unlikely that he can see what I saw.

I feel oddly empty when I realise that I can't tell anyone, except maybe Kate and Bonnie. What good is this information if I can't even talk about it? What am I supposed to do with it?

He gives me another one of his warm, patient smiles, and I feel like I've passed his test.

'I believe that, too.'

My heart warms. It feels good when you're honest with someone and find they share your world view.

He puts the books in a bag and hands it to me. 'That's twenty-five pounds.'

I stare at the bag a second. I'm sure the encyclopaedia alone was twenty pounds.

'I thought it'd be closer to fifty.'

He nods. 'Curiosity should be encouraged. The big one is on me.'

'Oh no, I can't accept that.' I rummage around in my purse for the rest of the cash.

'Consider it a down payment, then,' he says. 'If you find anything in there that you'd like to know more about, you know where to find the books.'

I laugh, but it comes out awkward. 'Well then, thank you,

erm…'

I automatically went to say his name, but of course, I don't know it.

'Leverett,' he says. 'Leverett Ilves.'

My awkwardness is gone when I smile again. Mum always said that I'm better at making friends older than myself. Something about people my age being too childish.

'Esta Anderson.' I pick up the bag. 'I'd better go put these to good use.'

I don't know why it sounds so cringy, but I wish I'd stopped after my name.

CHAPTER
FIVE

Lady is her usual happy puppy-self when we arrive at home, but I'm a sweaty mess full of regrets. It's much too hot to be carrying anything, let alone three heavy books. The bag helps, but about five minutes into my walk home I had no idea how to position it. It was too heavy in my hands, and welts were forming on my fingers. It was too tight around my wrists. The handle isn't long enough for me to sling it over my shoulder. I don't know why people pay for gym memberships when all you need is a big-as-fuck book and a weak bag. I never needed a shower more.

Lady runs straight for her water bowl, and I struggle up the stairs. I toss my clothes into my laundry basket, and then I close my eyes in gratitude as the cold water washes away the sweat. Bonnie still isn't back and she'll shower at the pool, anyway, so I'm content to take my time.

At least, that was my plan while I was still walking—to spend the rest of my life in a cold shower while eating ice cream. Logic doesn't apply when you're melting. Now that I'm home and already feeling better after two minutes under the water, I want more than anything to start reading. I have a lot of material to get through, and there's even more waiting for me at the bookshop—at *Leverett*'s shop. I mustn't forget his name.

I wrap myself in a towel and sit cross-legged on my bed. It won't take five minutes until I'm air-dried and sweating again. Part of me already misses the shower. A much larger part of me is eyeing the books like sweets, wondering what I should devour first. *The Super-Natural in Ancient History* and *Living Among Us—Stories of the Paranormal* would make more sense, probably, but I can't keep my eyes off the encyclopaedia. If everything in there is real…

It's a much bigger world than I ever knew.

I begin to leaf through it. It's very exciting for a few seconds before it becomes overwhelming. There is *so much* information. How am I supposed to internalise any of this in one morning? I know I have longer since the book is mine now, but I kind of wish I had a deadline and one specific goal so I wasn't aimlessly wandering through the pages.

I've seen more fairies than anything else. That's assuming that they *are* fairies, though. I could be wrong. I don't really know anything except that I wasn't aware any of this existed until I jumped into the void lake. They've been hiding rather successfully from humanity for… well, possibly forever. What if everything we see on TV and read in novels is part of their hiding strategy? They could have been feeding us lies on purpose for all I know.

I take a moment to breathe. That's not a slope I want to slip on. I don't know how they're hiding or if that's even what's happening, but there must be some reason why no one else can see them—*if* it's everyone else—and why I can see them now. I hate making assumptions, and assuming the worst of someone is even, well, worse. The void lake has something to do with this, so maybe I should start there.

I open *The Collective Unconscious* next, but I have a feeling I can't just dip in, get the info I want, and be done with it. Chances are I'll have to read the whole book and draw my own conclusions... which is great, because I love doing that kind of research, but I want something I can use *now*. I want at least a few answers. I have the rest of my life to read these books and fine-tune my research, and I don't suppose the fairies, demons, and all those other species are going anywhere.

Maybe I should start with what to call them. Is there a collective term? *Species* and *race* sound wrong. I don't want to use anything that might be derogatory. The book titles refer to them as "Super-Natural" and "Paranormal," but I don't know if those umbrella terms are too vague. If I knew one of them, I could ask, but I don't, so...

Unless Kate knows. She's a witch, so not quite the same as a fairy or a werewolf—she can't throw fireballs across the room unless she picks up a torch and chucks that across the space—but she probably knows more than I do. She's already expecting me to talk to her about scrying, anyway. After everything that's happened, I'm not sure it's still a priority, although if it explains what happened with the lake, I'm all in.

I leave the books on my bedside table and go into the garden. Kate often works on her herb garden, and I find her

60

there today, too. Her dogs are lounging in the shade.

She waves and smiles when she sees me. 'How are you?'

I return a nervous smile. 'A little confused, to be honest. Do you have a moment?'

She sets her gardening tools aside and waves me over. 'You mentioned scrying. Is that what you're confused about?'

I cock my head. 'Maybe.'

'Alright. This sounds interesting. Make yourself comfortable'—she nods to her small outdoor seating area—'and I'll get us some iced teas.'

I hop over the wall, get comfy in one of the chairs, and close my eyes while I wait. Her dogs looked up when I jumped over, but they're too comfy in the shade to move. They know me, and that's good enough for them. I let my head fall back a little and feel the breeze on my face. The seats and table are under a large willow tree, so I'm not baking in the sun.

Kate joins me with the drinks, complete with ice cubes and straws, and sits opposite me.

'So, maybe scrying?' she asks.

I sip my iced tea while I consider how to phrase it. Kate is the last person who would judge me, but that doesn't mean she can read my mind. If the words come out badly and she doesn't know what I mean, we won't get anywhere.

It's sometimes hard to remember how individual dreams are. Something that makes sense to one person won't make any sense at all to someone else, and that's assuming the dreamer herself knows what the various signs mean. Most dreams use symbolism. I have arachnophobia, so spiders in my dreams might signify an unrealistic fear I have; it wouldn't mean the same to someone who adores spiders and keeps a few as beloved pets. Even though Kate and I have discussed dreams before and she has helped me understand a few, we're still separate people. There's a chance the void lake won't mean anything to her. If that's the case, I'll have to hope that Leverett has something helpful.

I'm mildly chuffed that I remember his name.

'There's a lake in my dreams I've never seen before,' I say. 'Mischief took me there a couple of nights ago, when I asked her to show me something new.'

I get hung up on the words. Something new... Well, the fairies are definitely new. Did the lake somehow herald my discovery? But there was nothing particularly fairy-y about it, let alone angelic or demonic. I feel like I'm sort of close, like a word that's on the tip of my tongue. It bugs me that I can't quite grasp it.

'Did Mischief know it was there?' Kate asks.

I nearly say *yes*, but then I shake my head. 'We both felt drawn towards it, but we didn't know what it was until we got there.'

Kate nods. 'Perhaps because your request wasn't specific. When you have a large cupboard with many drawers, you won't know what's inside until you open them, but you can still decide to try one you've never opened before.'

I'm so lucky she's my neighbour. The way she explains things makes everything sound so simple, at least to me. I don't understand the void lake, but I can picture her metaphor.

'It was black, but not completely,' I say. 'It reminded me of the night sky, or maybe space. When I touched it, it was silky smooth and cool. Not cold, though. Does that make sense?'

Kate nods for me to continue.

'When I went in…' I bite my lip. If Kate can't see the supernaturals—and I think it's safe to assume that she can't—will she believe me? 'I didn't think anything had happened. I felt like I was floating through the galaxy, or like I was part of it. I felt… like myself? At peace. But that was all, until I got up and took Lady for a walk. I saw… Erm…' I gulp. Moment of truth and bravery, here I come. 'Well, I think I saw fairies. And demons. And maybe angels.'

It sounds ridiculous. I glance up from my straw, my heart hammering. But Kate looks her usual non-judgemental kind of interested, and it makes me feel better. Even if she doesn't believe it, she doesn't dismiss me.

'That's…'

I brace myself.

'It's unexpected, Esta. I didn't think…' Her eyes glaze over for a moment. 'And you're not scared?'

I shake my head, but my heart misses a few beats. She doesn't sound surprised. Why isn't she surprised? 'A little overwhelmed, maybe. To be honest, I don't know what to do with the information.'

'That's only natural,' she says. 'I'm impressed that you're not in shock, but I can't say I'm surprised. You never judged me when I told you that I practice witchcraft.'

I dislike labels because they complicate things. To many people, the term means that she worships Satan and sacrifices children, when really she grows herbs and owns a few tarot decks. That's not all she does, of course, but it's pretty tame compared to some people's fears.

Encouraged by her acceptance, I decide to say a little more. 'I sat in the park this morning. There were so many, but none of them cared that I was there. No one tried to hurt me. This little girl with a tail came up to me to retrieve her ball, and she seemed perfectly lovely.' For a kid, anyway. 'You're taking this well.'

This has been their normality for their whole lives and their ancestors' lives. Nothing has changed for them; my perception has. That's all it is. But that doesn't explain Kate's reaction.

'I see them, too, though I may not see as much as you,' Kate says.

My heart misses another beat—any more revelations and I might pass out. Frankly, maybe I should have seen this one coming. Of course Kate knows. If anyone did, it would be her.

Her eyes grow wary. 'Many have revealed themselves to me when they realised I'm no threat. I recommend you don't tell them that you know. They're not used to it. Some might not react well.'

A shiver runs down my arms despite the heat and despite my relief that I'm not entirely alone. I had no intention of running up to the fairy family and shouting their secret to the world, but the warning still gives me pause.

'What does it have to do with my dream?' I ask.

Kate regards me for a moment. 'Truthfully, I don't know, but this is a good thing.' The way she hesitated makes me think that she does know, but if she does and isn't telling me, she has her reasons. She always does. I can trust that. 'Your view of the world is expanding. Embrace it, but be cautious as you discover more. As I said, they're not used to people they don't know uncovering their true identities. Parents especially will be protective of their children.'

'I promise I won't say anything.' I bite my lip again. 'What about Bonnie? Oh, and I went to that bookshop you recommended. I think the owner might be alright—he seems very open-minded.' It'll make my research a hell of a lot easier if I don't have to talk around what I want.

Kate sips her tea. 'You know who you trust, but consider before you tell either of them that your words affect more people than yourself. It might be better to gently test their open-mindedness instead of being blunt.'

I couldn't agree more.

I didn't exactly doubt what I saw, but hearing Kate talk about it too makes me feel a little better. There was still that niggle of self-doubt, a little voice telling me I was imagining things, even if I didn't acknowledge it. That Kate knows this big secret I can in no way talk about is reassuring. It's also nice to know that, even if I don't tell Bonnie and Leverett, I can still talk to Kate. At least I'm not alone.

'What should I do?' I ask. 'You said to be cautious and to embrace it, but I don't know how. I can't just pretend that I don't see them.' And what about my photography project idea? That'll need some thought. 'How can I embrace it without giving anything away?'

Kate thinks for a moment as she finishes her tea. It's nice that little old me can still give a seasoned witch pause.

'Observe for now. Perhaps you already know people who

aren't human and you never realised. If you do, they would be the easiest starting point. Family won't be as defensive as a stranger might be.'

No one comes to mind. I'll be damned if any of my relatives have been demons all along. Some I don't exactly love, sure, but demons? That seems like a stretch.

Not that all demons are necessarily evil, as I've just learned. All of this will take some getting used to, or rather, my thinking will need some shifting.

'I doubt it, but thank you. I'll keep an eye out?' It doesn't really work unless I visit my family up north, and that's not how I was hoping to spend the summer. Although… What if I'm the last person to find out? What if my parents already know and just never told me? It's possible—it took them twenty-five years to casually mention that my dad is Estonian. How many more lies have you fed me, Mother? I don't suppose I'll ever know, since I'm not sure how I'd ask. I'll either never know or I'll find out at the next family party, and I make an effort not to go to those. My family consists of party people, and that's not me.

'Let me know if you have more questions,' Kate says.

I thank her and excuse myself. This morning has been a lot. I really fancy some me-time, maybe with a peppermint tea and my new encyclopaedia.

And then, when Bonnie comes home, I can casually ask her if she's seen any angels lately.

CHAPTER
SIX

I'm sprawled out on my bed when I hear Bonnie's key in the door. The room looks like a war zone, as my overly dramatic mum would say, all because I've got a few clothes on the floor and four open books on my bed. There are also two notebooks, one with photography ideas and one for everything I've learned today, just in case I forget any of it. And a fineliner and a fountain pen. The latter leaked all over my duvet some months ago. The stain is still there, and I have accepted that it's never coming out. To my mum, this duvet would now be something to throw out, like one small ink spot makes it unusable. To me, it adds character, like the stain is now part of my bed's history and says that a person with too many notebooks lives here.

Bonnie's footsteps echo up the walls as she runs up the staircase—if she can turn a regular everyday moment into exercise, she will. I look up when she knocks and pokes her head into my room. Her hair has dried in messy strands. It gives her a surfer vibe even though she's never stood on a surfboard. She'll comb it out and smooth it with some nourishing hair cream. I almost never bother, but she needs the control after her chaotic childhood. We're both control freaks in our own way.

'How was your swim?' I ask.

She glances over the books on the bed. 'Good! It was busy, but I managed. Didn't swim into anyone.' It's more likely that the other visitors cleared a path for her. My sister is a power swimmer. 'You have a good morning?'

I roll over and wince when I roll straight onto a sharp hardback corner.

'Until now! Ouch.' I sit up so the offending book can't hurt me again. 'I took Lady for her walk and went back to the book shop.'

She nods like it brings order to the chaos on my bed. 'That explains all the books! I was wondering if you fancied an ice cream, but if you're busy…'

I'm on my feet within seconds. 'No, let's do that.'

She was out longer than I thought. It's gone lunch time, and I've been reading for about an hour. Because there's so much to take in, my head feels like it's melted. A break will be nice, and talking to her like this—casually, like nothing has changed—makes it easy to switch off for a moment.

I follow her downstairs but pause halfway down. 'Wait. Didn't we finish the last box?'

She puts on her shoes. 'I thought we could go to the pub. I've been wanting to try their sundaes for weeks.'

I hum in agreement. Our local pub is only about eight minutes down the road, and they have this wicked sundae with tons of fruit, chocolate, biscuits, and chocolate sauce. It sounds like a dream, and there's a sharing option.

Lady is watching us very carefully from the sofa.

'Wanna come?' Bonnie asks.

'They'll have a bowl of water for you,' I add.

Lady barks and throws herself towards us, stumbling over her own paws a little. Bless her, she's so easily pleased.

Bonnie fastens the leash to Lady's collar and we're on our way.

We're fortunate to live in a quiet neighbourhood with a park across the road but without losing any of the benefits of city life. We have an airport nearby, a train station, and even a port where cruise ships dock. The airport and train station are small—we have two gates and two platforms—but they are there. We can go pretty much anywhere from here. The walk to the pub takes us along the busy main road, which isn't very scenic, but I'm okay with that if it means I get my ice cream sooner.

I'm always surprised that so many people brave the heat. I would happily stay inside where the sunshine can't burn my pale skin, but several groups of sun worshippers pass us on the way. Bonnie would drag me to the beach every weekend if I let her. Maybe now I'm off for the summer I'll make an exception for her. She can swim and Lady and I can lounge under a parasol with a book. I wonder if all supernaturals go to the beach. Vampires probably don't since, you know, sunshine, and werewolves have all that fur which has got to get too hot, but I can picture fairies playing with beach balls and splashing in the water. Maybe a visit to the beach wouldn't be too bad if it means I can people-watch—if anyone asks, I can always use the very true excuse that I'm a photographer and therefore love observing people.

The pub has only been open since lunch, but the garden is already filling up. Lady and I snatch a table near the river while Bonnie orders our sundaes. She joins us with a bowl for Lady.

I love this place. It's relaxing, with the river hugging one side and the tree canopies overhead; just what I need after my morning. I keep my eyes on the river while Bonnie orders—if possible, I'd love this moment to just *be* with my sister. No people watching. No supernatural noticing. Just a normal day out.

Bonnie puts her sunglasses on the table. 'Are you better now?'

'Was I sick earlier?' I ask.

'You know, because of that lake. You seemed disappointed this morning.'

I swallow. I know I can tell her anything, but here? One look around the other visitors doesn't reveal too much, though I'm sure two guys opposite us have wings. It's surprisingly hard to tell since they don't have their backs to me and I try not to stare at anyone. Kate's warning echoes in my mind—they might not be happy that I know, especially since we're strangers. And what if…

What if there are others like me who know and want to be rid of them? Witch hunts happened. I can't really call them *witch* hunters if they hunt fairies and demons instead, but if some humans do know, I bet those people exist, too. I don't want to talk about it in a place where anyone can overhear and possibly take offense, and I really don't want to shout it around if those kinds of people might be listening for hints. Maybe that's why the supernaturals are hiding.

A frustrated sigh escapes me. I know so little, but who can I ask?

'Alright,' Bonnie says. 'Let's talk about it?'

I smile, more disappointed than ever that I have this information and can do absolutely fuck all with it.

'No, it's fine,' I say. 'I was upset this morning, but I'm over it. Ever had a dream that lingered after you woke up, like it was more profound somehow?'

Bonnie stares at me like I spoke another language.

I laugh. I suppose she wouldn't know.

'Well, it's like that. Like when you watch a horror film and jump at every shadow for a few days afterwards.'

A sparkle enters her eyes, and she giggles. We're both massive cowards, but unlike me, she loves watching horror movies. I watch with her because, while I hate being terrified, I love our movie nights, and the fear isn't so bad when we both jump so severely that our popcorn goes flying and we find popped kernels days later. The ones Lady couldn't reach, anyway.

Bonnie's eyes go wide. 'Wait, so you're saying your dream was like a nightmare? That doesn't sound nice.'

Our sundae arrives—Bonnie opted for the massive sharing option. I get distracted by the horns coming out of the waitress's head and stare a little too long.

She winks at me. 'It's my birthday. I can wear what I want.'

Bonnie and I laugh, but I silently chide myself for staring. What if they weren't made of plastic? Do I really want to worry a demon? No, thank you.

'Too right,' I say.

She leaves us to enjoy our ice cream, and Bonnie sighs.

'I hope I get a boss this lenient. Your manager and the people here seem so relaxed if they let her wear that.'

I nod. I did get super lucky. 'Did I tell you about that time my colleague turned forty and dressed as a unicorn?'

Bonnie chokes on a frozen-solid chocolate cookie. 'No. Please, go on.'

'She turned forty and dressed as a unicorn.' I laugh at her *well, duh!* expression. 'She wore a tail and a horn, and on her lunch break she galloped through the gallery. Many of the staff joined her.'

Bonnie raises an eyebrow. 'Did you?'

I shake my head, not sure if I'm relieved or sad that I missed out. 'Her birthday is during my summer break, so I wasn't there for it. I've seen pictures, though, and someone recorded it.'

'Can I come work with you when I've graduated?'

Honestly, I would love nothing more.

'You probably could,' I say, 'but we both know you need the ocean to be happy. If anything, I'll move with you when you go to Brighton or somewhere exotic to study tropical marine life.'

She sighs again with a blissful smile. 'We could get one of those houses by the beach, in the suburbs.'

One weekend we stupidly drove to Brighton—the city is a nightmare to navigate. We've taken the train every time since. It's a bit of a hassle since we need to change twice, sometimes three times, but it beats the stress of getting lost in an unfamiliar city with too many one-way roads any day. We did find this nice neighbourhood near the beach, though. You can see the sea from there, and the walk to the beach is shorter than the walk to the pub today. It was paradise... apart from getting lost and angry at the roads.

We stay in the pub for nearly an hour after finishing the sundae. Lady got comfy on the ground and has shut her eyes. I want to tell Bonnie everything, but not here. Not now. I know she'll prefer proof, but there's nothing I can offer her besides my word and Kate's. I know she'd believe me, but proof is better. If I could get a picture... If I'm to base my next photography project around this, I'll need to figure out a way to photograph them without getting them or myself into trouble. I probably can't just walk up to one and say, 'Hey, I see you're a fairy. I'm a photographer. Your wings are beautiful—mind if I take some pictures?' I don't see that going well.

An idea begins to form in my head, but it's like a dream— if I try too hard to figure out the details, it'll vanish forever. I need a little more time to let it simmer.

But when we leave the pub and stroll home, I feel less frustrated and more excited. This can be The Project. I just need to be careful.

CHAPTER
SEVEN

I close my eyes and hug my first tea of the day with both hands while the morning's breeze brushes over me. The early-morning peace of our garden is everything to me, and I appreciate it today especially. I spent the weekend reading my new books. The more I read, the more I realised how much more there is to the world. It's exciting, but it's also overwhelming. Fairies alone are so much more complex than I knew.

For one, I should probably be calling them fae. From there, a million branches exist. Okay, not one million, but are we in the double digits? Easily. There are sylphs, elves, pixies, gnomes… And that's *just* the fae. There are also werewolves, mermaids, vampires—the ones everyone's heard of. I've also read about brownies and boggarts in this book, banshees—another kind of fae—sirens, ghosts, all kinds of spirits, actual unicorns, bloody titans and dragons, and let's not even start with demons. They have as many, if not more, subcategories as the fae. And then there are *gods*.

Unless not everything in this book is true, but how the hell am I supposed to know the difference anymore?

So, by the time the weekend is over, my head feels ready to split.

I have as many photography ideas as there are fae and demons combined, and I've no idea where to start. The more I read over the weekend, the more I know I can't just walk up to someone and ask to photograph their wings or tails or whatever. I rarely photograph people I don't know. I've always felt awkward walking up to strangers and saying, 'I think you look interesting, can I photograph you?' When I was still a student, many of my peers approached their work that way, but that's not me and I can't see it ever being me. I'm way too socially awkward. I'd probably blurt out 'Nice horns!' for the whole high street to hear, which isn't a good way to start a friendship with a demon who wants to stay hidden.

But I don't like the idea of just photographing them like they're part of the scenery, either. I've always felt awkward doing that. It's why I am my own subject so often. Self-portraiture has its own struggles, but I prefer the difficulties of being a self-conscious kitten to shoving my camera at strangers. At least when it's just me, I can take my time.

And all that only works if any of them would even show in the images. I've taken a lot of pictures over the years, and many have people in them, even if they aren't the focus. Some of them must have been supernatural, and no one ever saw anything more than random humans in the pictures. There have been a few exceptions over the years, but those photographs have always been highly disputed. Some people saw what the photographer saw, others called them frauds and either accused them of manipulating the images or of reading too much into shadows and sun rays. All artists know that you can't please everyone, but with projects like this, I genuinely don't know what to expect.

Even if I did get an angel's permission to flaunt their wings for my camera, I might still be the only one who can tell. Everyone else might look at the picture and see someone's bare back. What if that ends my career before it has a chance to take off? And what if people *would* see what I see? From what Kate said, the supernatural community wouldn't want that, which takes me back to zero.

So, I made loads of progress over the weekend while also getting nowhere.

I'm not giving up, though. I wanted something big for this project, and now I have it. All I need is to find a way to make it work. Ethically or not at all.

Something hits my arm, and I jump. Tea spills onto my wrist and legs. Fortunately, it's cooled too much to burn me, but I still squeal.

Bonnie covers her mouth like she's sorry she made me jump, but her shoulders shake with withheld giggles. 'Oops! Earth to Esta. You didn't burn yourself, did you?'

I smirk. 'Nuh. I got too lost in thought, so this'—I wave the mug at her—'is cold. Sorry. Did you say something?'

She sits on the crumbling low wall, which effectively splits our garden in two, and crosses her legs. 'I was just asking what you're up to today. They're offering snorkelling lessons at Bournemouth beach and I really want to go. Wanna come?'

I raise an eyebrow. 'I think you know the answer to that.'

She nudges me playfully. 'So, what will you do? More research?'

It's tempting, but I don't think my head can take much more.

'I might go back to the book shop.' His name is Leverett—*yes*, I still remember it. I'd high-five myself if it wouldn't look so sad. 'I'm not sure what I'm looking for, but I'll know it when I see it.'

'I can help you search if you like?'

I do love browsing books with my sister. It's nice when we both get to fawn over pretty covers and hidden knowledge together, although the latter happens less often.

'Nuh, you go snorkelling,' I say. 'I'd never come between you and the open ocean.'

She rolls her eyes. 'Well, duh, you'd drown!'

We laugh and I nudge her back.

'I'll take Lady with me,' she says. 'The website says that people are encouraged to bring their dogs, so hopefully she won't be the only one there.'

I laugh. 'And to think I was worried you'd just stay in the ocean and I'd never see you again! Turns out, we're more at risk of losing Lady forever.'

Lady loves the beach, probably because she doesn't get to go very often. We do have a beach here, but it's not within walking distance, and when I work and Bonnie is at uni, there isn't much time to drive somewhere just for a walk. Lady reverts to a puppy when she smells the sea and feels sand under her paws. Since Bonnie loves the ocean as much as I love books, I know they'll both have the best day together.

For a moment, I'm tempted to join them after all. My boss once—alright, many times—told me that I work too much and should take more days off. I know she has a point, but it's not like I'm working every day in some job I loathe with every fibre of my being. The gallery isn't my endgame, but it's not that bad, and I love working on my photography, so that's not work, either. I mean, it is—I literally want it to be my career— but it's not like a dead-end office job I hate. Most of the people I've talked to liken *work* to *I hate everything about this situation and am a perma-stressed pigeon*, and my photography isn't that. Work can be enjoyable.

'Have fun,' I say. As much as I love my sister, there's no power in the universe strong enough to convince me to put my head underwater in an open ocean. Nightmares are made from that stuff, and most of them originate from me.

Lady throws herself into Bonnie's car, and I wave as they drive past me. I've got a license, but unlike me, Bonnie actually likes driving and is much better at it, so it may as well be her car despite being in both of our names.

I'm grateful that the weather has cooled down a bit. Maybe there's an end to this heatwave in sight. Maybe even a storm, some thunder. Or a lot of thunder.

I *love* thunder. Most people I know aren't keen on it, but to me, it's almost as relaxing as standing outside in high winds. Almost.

Right now, though, it's still hot, just not as hot. Clouds have begun to move in, and I hope to every star in the universe that they'll hurry up and drop a million buckets of rain on us already.

It's hard to stay focussed on my walk. Thanks to the heat, the entire city seems to be out and basking in the sunshine. I try hard not to stare, but I also want to take in everything. Not wanting to be rude and potentially piss off some dangerous angels, I focus on my feet. Maybe I can find a book about blending in with the supernatural community or the diary of someone who did just that.

I breathe a sigh of relief when I reach the book shop— because it's easier to not stare when I'm the only customer, because the air con is divine, and because I'll never not sigh at old-book smell.

The little bell rings when I enter, but I don't see Leverett. He must have figured that, since there's no one on the shop floor, he's okay to do whatever he does in the back. The sign says it's open and the door wasn't locked, so I shrug and head straight for the shelves he showed me last time.

If this place had a sofa or an armchair, he'd never get rid of me. Maybe he wouldn't mind if I grabbed a stack and got comfy in the back? I'll sit on some boxes if I have to.

'Back again?'

I jump and yelp. Leverett is right next to me. Where the hell did he come from? First Bonnie and now him—it should be illegal to move this quietly.

He chuckles. 'I'm sorry, I didn't think you were so absorbed in…' He bends his neck to read the cover. '…*Occult Philosophy.*'

I blush. 'I'm not, I just didn't hear you. I didn't think you were on the shop floor.'

His smile warms, and I feel stupid for jumping. Really, what did I expect? I know he works here. Even if this were my first visit and we hadn't met yet, someone had to be working here.

'Then I'm sorry I made you jump. Can I help you find anything?'

I smile back. 'Apology accepted.'

Can I tell him? He hasn't given me any reason to think that he'd judge me for what I saw—still see, if I take one look outside the shop. Kate recommended this shop, albeit for the selection. She did also warn me to be careful, but it's not like I'm taking a megaphone and announcing the fairies' names and addresses to the city. It's just him, and...

I think I can trust him.

Still, I feel nervous when I phrase my question. 'I've noticed some...' I swallow. I didn't think it'd be this hard. Forever a fan of just ripping the plaster off, I say, 'I saw some fairies and demons in my local park and was hoping to find another book of similar encounters.'

I was calmer in the second half of that sentence, right until *similar encounters*. Now I just sound stuffy.

Leverett doesn't speak for a moment, and I worry I've overstepped a line. I glance at him. There's something odd in his eyes. Not confusion—well, maybe a little—or disbelief— okay, maybe a little of that, too—but at least it's not the *I can't believe you're such an airhead* look.

'Do you have anything?' I ask. My heart races faster the longer he's quiet.

'I might. I think there's something in the back, now that I think about it, but it might be too much.'

Now it's my turn to look confused. 'Too much as in too much information or too much to carry?'

The way he said it made a shiver run down my back. He smiles again, and my worries gently fall away.

'Something like that.'

'Consider me intrigued,' I say. 'I'll wait h—'

He intently looks at me like he's waiting for me to say something else, but I don't realise what until he smiles just a little and I see his teeth—sorry, his fangs.

He's a vampire.

I guess.

Or maybe a demon, or—

My heart races faster, and I can literally feel myself pale. This shouldn't be a big deal. I saw all those other people and was perfectly happy to watch them.

They weren't this close to me, though. And we weren't alone in an empty book shop, either.

I don't know him at all. Kate's words echo in my head again. What if he isn't happy that I know?

Shit. What have I walked into?

He chuckles, and my knees go weak. It doesn't sound evil or predatory. I just hope it's not a 'Haha, trapped you!' kind of laugh. It really doesn't sound like it, but then, what do I know? Not much, evidently.

'I apologise,' he says. 'I was curious to see how you'd react. Every now and again someone thinks they've seen a fairy when they've really just seen a trick of the light, and people these days use the term *demon* too casually for it to hold much weight.'

His casual tone helps me relax. If he wanted to hurt me, he's had plenty of chances since this shop isn't exactly a hotspot.

He could probably charm me or lure me into the back and kill me there without anyone on the high street noticing. But he hasn't. In fact, he's been nothing but nice to me.

'Sorry,' I say. 'I didn't mean to…' What? I didn't mean to go pale? '… stare.'

'It's quite natural to be afraid when confronted with a predator. I'm not offended.'

I swallow. 'Good. I mean, I'm glad.' Am I rambling? I feel like I'm rambling. 'I mean, I like coming here, so…'

I'll shut up now before I dig myself a grave I can't crawl out of.

'I read that supernaturals wouldn't like me knowing what they are, so I wasn't afraid, I just wasn't sure.' *Keep digging, Esta.* At least I managed to talk around Kate. No need to drag her into this. 'Not that you'd have shown me your— As you said, you're not offended, so…'

Being a social butterfly is not one of my strengths. I excel at social awkwardness instead.

'I won't tell anyone,' I say. 'Not that anyone would believe me, but I promise I won't.'

'Relax,' Leverett says. 'I assure you I have no intention of silencing you now that you know my terrible secret.' He chuckles again, and a nervous laugh escapes me. If I could stop being an idiot now, that'd be great. 'But I am rather curious as to how you came to this power. Most of us go to great lengths to stay hidden. In that regard, you're quite right to be nervous.'

I'm not sure where to start unpacking that.

'Why did you show me if you don't want anyone to know?' I ask.

'I'd like to think myself a good judge of character. If I thought you'd be a danger to my existence, I wouldn't have revealed myself to you.'

I nod. 'Thank you, then. For trusting me.'

He returns the nod. 'May I ask you a few questions?'

I laugh, less nervous this time. '*You* have questions for *me*? I don't know if I can answer them, but go ahead.'

He waves to the back of the shop. 'Would you like a tea? I have a feeling this will be a long talk, and you look like you could use a drink.'

Well, it'd be rude to say no to free tea. My mama raised me better than that.

Although the idea of sitting alone with a vampire in the back of his shop makes my heart beat faster again. If he's asking me questions, it's only fair that I get to ask him some of my own. I might actually get some answers today.

'I'll never say no to tea,' I say.

I sit on a crate amidst boxes and more crates while Leverett is upstairs rummaging through what I imagine to be a kitchen. It's obvious that he's only just moved in—there's no real order to any of it, at least none that I can see. I've peeked into a few of the boxes and found books, books, and books. Some look much older than the ones I saw on the shop floor.

I also had a glance around for a coffin, but as far as I can tell, there isn't one, at least not down here. The flat upstairs seems to be his, so it makes sense that everything more personal would be there, away from the shop. I try to remember if the windows looked tinted or if the curtains have been drawn every time I've walked past, but I've no idea. I so rarely look up when I walk, and even then I don't normally have a reason to pay attention to details like that.

Leverett returns with two cups of tea. I smell the peppermint before he hands me the cup. I close my eyes and inhale while he sits on another crate opposite me.

'Which brand is this?' I ask. 'I've tried a few, but none have smelled this good.'

I'll be buying fifty boxes on the way home, please and thank you.

'You wouldn't have found this one on any supermarket shelf or even online,' he says. 'I grow my own herbs and create my own infusions. If you like this one, you're welcome to take a bag home.'

I wave him off. 'I'd love one, but I'll pay for it.' It smells to divine not to.

'Consider our discussion ample payment, if you like.'

I smile into my cup and nod. 'Then I wish I had better answers, but I don't really know what happened.' Given how honest he was with me a moment ago, all my reservations have died. He's trusting me with a big secret, and I'm happy to do the same. 'Remember when I came in looking for books about scrying?'

He nods.

'I found a lake in my dreams I've never seen before—I've had lucid dreams since I was a child, so I haven't found anything new in a while. I felt drawn to it, went in, and next thing I know, every other person has either wings or tails or both.'

A gross under-description, but Leverett nods like it makes perfect sense to him.

'Curious,' he says. 'I've never heard of such a lake, but as I'm sure you're aware, everyone's dreamscape is different.'

'Do vampires dream?' I freeze, and my heart hammers. 'If that's not a rude question. Don't answer if I shouldn't have asked.'

'Not at all. We don't need sleep like you do. By extension, we don't have many opportunities to dream. As I mentioned outside, you might consider us predators, so we sleep with one eye open, if you will. It's closer to deep relaxation than sleep.'

I nod. I've struggled to fall asleep at times and felt like I was dreaming while also being half-awake. I wonder if it's similar.

'May I ask what you intend to do with your new knowledge?'

Is that a hint of nervousness from him? He regards me carefully like my answer is important, but I already promised not to tell anyone.

'I don't know,' I say. 'Honestly, I don't know what I *can* do with it. I'd love to do a photography project, but I don't know how to approach it.'

His expression is weary. 'Be careful if you go in that direction. You mentioned reading that we want to stay hidden, and there's good reason for our caution.'

I sit a little straighter. 'Why is that?'

He looks deep in thought as he sips his tea—I imagine he got himself one, too; could be blood, I don't know—and regards me like he's considering how much he can tell me.

'We have always shared this planet,' he says. 'Some of us,

like vampires and fairies, live for a very long time. We have no need to reproduce fast. Humans, however, never had that luxury. You quickly overtook us in numbers.'

I have so many questions but I don't want to interrupt, so I save them for later.

'At first, we got along, or many of us did. But as humans grew larger in numbers, you were less interested in friendship and more interested in ruling. You figured there were more of you—why shouldn't you rule everyone? What's more, many of us supernaturals, as you called us, didn't develop at the rates humans did. Fairies, for example, outright shun technology. Because we had lived in peace for so long, humans didn't realise what a war would cost them.'

He finished his tea.

'We never wanted to fight you, but we defended ourselves. We didn't see why any one species should rule all others when we were all so different and had managed individually for so long, but you humans need to control and change everything you see.'

He sneers like I've opened an ancient wound. I wish I hadn't asked, but I'm beginning to understand their caution.

'There was a war. Many of us died, but the humans had heavy losses, too. War is your nature, not ours, so we decided to make you forget we exist. None of us can work magic that powerful, however, so we looked to different solutions. We vampires, for example, can easily hide our fangs and blend in. At most, we have to move to other places every now and again or else people get suspicious when we don't age. Others, like fairies, can't just tug their wings away or make them disappear, so they use charms to make them appear invisible.

'It wasn't our first choice, but it's the only way to preserve the balance. To my knowledge, some haven't tried to blend in. Sirens and mermaids, for example, live in environments that aren't habitable to humans, so they simply retreated to their underwater kingdoms.

'This is why I'd like to repeat again that dedicating a photography project to us wouldn't be wise. Many might see it as an act of aggression.'

A shiver runs down my spine, arms, toes. Here I was, worried that they might not like it; but war? That's the last thing I want.

'No, absolutely not,' I say. 'I mean, I want peace, too. But if some of you use charms to hide, why can I see through them?'

A smile tugs at his lips like I passed a test. 'That's the question. You don't remember anything else about the lake?'

I shake my head. 'But maybe I don't need to. It might not matter. What I do with it is more important, isn't it?'

He nods. 'Which brings me back to my earlier question. What do you intend to do with your new knowledge?'

I still want to do that photography project, but not if it causes a war. So much time has passed. Surely we could learn to coexist?

I frown. 'Hang on. You said you decided to erase yourselves from our memories, but you're everywhere—in movies, TV shows, books, you name it. How is that hiding?'

He chuckles. 'Just a bit of cautious fun, if you will. Much of what you find in popular media is exaggerated, but it keeps humans preoccupied and careful. If everyone expects you to only show up at night and be repulsed by garlic, it's easier to blend in during the day and eat food with garlic in it.'

I didn't even notice the time of day when he showed me his fangs.

'So, all of that is false?'

He nods. 'Not all of it, perhaps, but most of it.'

Something has been playing on my mind since he started to tell me about the war. I ask it now.

'Couldn't vampires or werewolves, for example, easily outnumber humans by turning us into, well, you? Or is that a lie, too?'

'It's not a lie.'

I go hot and cold. Apparently, I don't know how to handle that.

'It's not that simple, however,' he says. 'The risks of turning a human into a vampire are too high for most of us to attempt it. The results are… hard to control, if they survive.'

Movies always made it look so easy, but as I just learned, that's all lies.

'Why?' I ask. 'What happens?'

He glances at my cup. 'Would you like another tea?'

I didn't even notice it's empty. I doubt he knew for sure, but we've been talking for a while and I haven't exactly gone easy on it.

I shake my head. I'm afraid if I take in too much more information, my head will explode. After everything he has told me, I'm a little relieved that I'm talking to a vampire alone, not also to a bunch of other people. Part of me wishes I had brought a notebook, but I can't imagine I'll forget any of this.

'Thank you, but I'm fine,' I say. 'I'm sorry if I'm asking too many questions. I should have thought before the last one—it's probably sensitive information.'

He shakes his head. His smile is still there, so I don't think I offended him.

'It's... refreshing, to talk so openly to a human. Conversations like this with your kind are rare.'

I raise an eyebrow. 'But you have talked to other humans?'

His smile disappears, and his eyes glaze over. 'On a few occasions. Most of them didn't end well.'

I nod. Sadly, I don't have any trouble believing that.

'Well,' I say, 'I promise I won't start a war. I've no intention of stepping on any... what do you call it? You said earlier "supernatural, as I call it," so you must have another term.'

Leverett shrugs. 'It's not a bad term, at least not by your definition—humans have always considered themselves the peak of everything. We're something other than them, so we've always been supernatural in your eyes. Really it's just another term for *unnatural*, though. For a while, you called us nonhumans. It's true, but you always put a derogatory edge to it.'

I want to apologise, but I wasn't even alive then. Whatever happened in their past, I had nothing to do with it. I'm here now, though. I will do better.

'So what should I call you?'

He thinks for a moment, then smiles again. 'Leverett would be nice.'

I smile back. 'I can do that. So, there's no collective term?'

'You could call us the Veiled,' he says. 'It's a term we

89

adopted a very long time ago.'

'Alright.' I nod, glad that I finally won't be stumbling over the correct terminology anymore. I smile wider. 'Nice to meet you, Leverett. I'm Esta.'

After everything he told me today, it feels right to introduce myself again.

He inclines his head. 'And you.'

'Thank you for being open with me,' I say. 'I'm only sorry that I learned so much while I had very little to tell you. It doesn't feel fair.'

He chuckles again. 'Oh, I wouldn't say that. Quite the contrary, in fact—I learned rather a lot about you through this conversation.'

I don't know what I could possibly have taught him, but if he's happy, that's good enough for me.

'Could I come back if I have more questions?' I don't want to smother him, but I also don't want to pass up the opportunity for answers. I do want peace, same as they do— it'll be harder to achieve that if we can't understand and accept each other. Leverett has been nothing but kind to me, so I'm more than happy to throw everything I thought I knew out the window and start again.

'You can come back any time you like.' He stands. 'I sense you're ready to go home and let all this sink in, so let me get you some of the tea to take with you.'

He disappears in a cloud of fog that flies up the stairs.

I sneer. 'Show-off!' I call after him.

In truth, I haven't blinked since he vanished. How would it feel to turn into fog? I can't imagine my body reassembling itself like that—well, I can imagine it visually, but how it would *feel?* I've no idea. I can only guess that it doesn't hurt him or he wouldn't do it, unless he really is just a show-off.

I watch as fog-Leverett flies back down and reappears before me. He hands me a bag of tea leaves like nothing happened.

'I have more if you want more.'

A slightly overwhelmed laugh escapes me. How can this be so... normal? I know it is for him, although... He did say he's not usually this open with humans, so it isn't all that normal for him, either.

So I remind myself not to stare and simply take the tea.

'Thank you.'

I hope he hears in my voice that I'm grateful for everything, not just the tea leaves.

CHAPTER
EIGHT

Since it's not as hot today and the breeze has picked up a little more, I decide to take my book outside. *The Collective Unconscious* calls to me, so I fill a glass with ice and peach iced tea and find a shady spot. The shade is great, the wind better, and the tea is lovely, but the book quickly becomes too much.

Or maybe it's more like the whole morning being a little much.

I'm grateful that Leverett answered so many questions, but I still feel like I'm missing something. Why me? Why now? What's the point of having all this knowledge, all this insight the Veiled are working so hard to keep from us, if I can't do anything with it? After my chat with Leverett, I was sure I couldn't do my photography project. It would bring too many people into the spotlight who do not want to be in the spotlight. But what if that's why I have this power? Maybe I'm supposed to shed some light on these hidden shadows. I don't really believe in destiny, but it's hard to make sense of all this without finding some kind of reason for it. Does everyone have a void lake in their dreamscape? Not everyone lucid dreams as freely as I do. Maybe that's why I found it, and not, say, my neighbour three doors down... who's probably a dryad or something equally magical, so they'd already know.

I sigh. It bugs me that I've gained this knowledge but am unable to use it. What if I could bring awareness to their community in a respectful way that brings humans and the Veiled together? Esta Anderson—Bringer of Peace, Uniter of People.

Yeah, I'm probably getting a little ahead of myself there.

But what if it's possible? What if photography could literally unite the world?

There's no point daydreaming that far ahead. I don't understand enough, and I'm already making a new list of questions to ask Leverett. I didn't ask if he drank tea with me or if he had blood instead. Of course, for all I know, that was a lie, too. Didn't he say something about eating garlic? If vampires can have regular Italian food, maybe they don't need blood at all.

He's been so open with me—with a secret he's apparently had bad experiences sharing—and I don't have anything comparable I can tell him. It doesn't seem fair, but then again, I can't help being a boring human.

Because the more I read, the more boring I feel and wish I'd been born as something else. Although, I'd have to hide my true nature, and that's not ideal, either. How would I feel if I had to wear plastic wings and pretend I'm a fairy because stars forbid anyone found out I'm human? All the more reason for me to be careful with my project, once I've figured out the right way to do it.

Given how few people believed that photographer when he published his images of fairies, chances are no one would believe me, anyway. Maybe this could be a way to show them that I know and support them without the humans catching on. But then what do I say when someone asks me about my inspiration?

Getting ahead of myself again. I'm not getting any reading done like this. *And* the ice has melted and watered down my drink.

'Hello, Esta.' Kate looks over the wall from her garden. Her eyes fall onto my book. 'Is this a bad moment?'

I shake my head and close the pages. 'No. I'm struggling to focus anyway.'

She leans onto the wall with her arms. 'I thought I'd see how you're doing. You had a lot on your mind last time.'

'Still do,' I say. 'If anything, I have more questions now.'

'Did you tell anyone else?'

Can I talk to her about Leverett? I didn't tell him about Kate.

I decide to keep to half-truths for now.

I get up and walk over to her. 'I told Leverett—the bookshop owner. He's... very open-minded.'

If Kate notices my hesitation, she doesn't react.

'He must have many interesting books in his collection,' she says.

I hold up *The Collective Unconscious*. 'I bought a few, including this one. I'll spend my whole salary in there if no one stops me.'

Kate laughs. 'It's nice to see you so willing to learn, but

don't read yourself into poverty. There are other ways to learn, too.'

I think of all the different people I saw in the park and wish, so much, that I could talk to just one of them.

'Observation only goes so far,' I say.

'This is true, but don't underestimate how far that is. Toddlers learn two whole languages through observation.'

I blink. 'Two?'

Kate nods. 'Verbal language and body language; although they do learn many words by asking questions, too. But wouldn't you agree that they learn more than enough by watching their caretakers?'

I've never really thought about it, but Kate is good at making me see things in new ways, of making me reconsider what I thought I knew. It's one of the things I treasure about her.

I give her a rueful smile. 'If only this were as easy as learning to talk.'

'Isn't it?' She straightens. 'Think of it as dance steps: It takes a lot of practice if you want to dance with the professionals, but if you keep trying and watching other dancers carefully, you'll improve and learn the right moves.'

I laugh. 'You've clearly never seen me dance!'

'Let's try this, then.' She nods to my apple tree. 'What do you see?'

I look it up and down, from its firm roots to its highest leaves. Flowers dot the crown. I'm already looking forward to baking apple crumbles and cakes, but I doubt that's what Kate has in mind.

I shrug. 'An apple tree.' I'm not sure what else she might want from me.

She walks across the lawn until she's just on the other side of the wall from it. 'Try to see beneath the bark. There's magic in this tree—life magic. All plants are filled with it, thrive because of it. You can't see it, but life flows up from the roots to the petals and leaves all the same. When you place your hand on the bark and feel the tree, you can sense some of that connection between all living things.'

I follow her and place my hand on the tree. It's cool and rough under my skin.

Kate looks up at the leaves with a proud smile, like she is its mother. 'All this has grown from one little seed, and it will continue to grow. Every apple that grows from it will in turn give us more seeds, which we can plant to grow yet more trees. Its potential is infinite. All living things share this potential.'

And she's lost me.

'I don't remember having any seeds to grow mini Estas.' But even as I say it, I realise how wrong I am. It's like I've never heard of children before.

Kate raises an eyebrow. 'I trust I don't have to educate you about human reproduction?'

I shake my head. 'No, I realised it while I was talking.'

She nods, pleased that I caught on.

'How does that help me?' I ask.

'What is knowledge if not another seed?' Kate says. 'You took one step by wading into the water—planting the seed, if you like—and now look at all the new knowledge—apples— you have gained from it. What more will you learn if you continue to cultivate your orchard?'

Her smile is mysterious; it's one of the many things I treasure about her. I love her comparison, too, but really it just leaves me with the same problem I've had before.

I let out a long, frustrated sigh. 'That's precisely where I'm stuck. I find myself in a garden with whole bags of seeds that I'm not supposed to plant.'

Kate cocks her head not unlike Lady. 'Who says you're not supposed to?'

I frown. 'You did. You said the Veiled wouldn't appreciate me knowing about them, and Leverett said the same thing.'

'Ah. This is true, but you misunderstood.' She leans forwards on the wall again. 'To return to the orchard comparison, consider the farmer who protects his land. He knows what the soil is capable of and what he can do with it. He's taken great care to look after it the best he knows how. You offer him an apple orchard, and he doesn't know what to make of it because the only apples he's ever tasted weren't grown with love and spoiled quickly. He doesn't believe it worth his effort. But perhaps, if you grow a tree with love away from his orchard and present to him a delicious apple, you might change his mind.'

I slowly nod, but really I'm still lost. 'This is getting confusing. I think I know what you're saying, but how can I show them that I know and am on their side if I can't approach them in the first place?'

That mysterious smile again. 'That is up to you, isn't it? Everyone is different. What works for me may not work for them. You need to trust your intuition when you take that step, but remember that you've already approached me, and you were honest with Leverett. Did either meeting have bad results?'

'No, but…' Kate never tried to hide from me—she was open about her practicing witchcraft from the beginning—and Leverett chose to reveal himself to me. Although… Now that I think about it, Kate didn't introduce herself with, 'My name is Kate and I'm a witch. Nice to meet you.' I saw her planting herbs and sitting under her tree one full moon, which made me comment that it looked relaxing. That's how we got talking and why she opened up. Leverett didn't reveal himself just because, either. He saw my interest and willingness to learn before he decided it was worth the risk. I didn't overthink either conversation, I was just being myself—asking questions and accepting the answers. Maybe that's how I need to approach this. It still won't be easy, but it's a start. I'll trust my gut and see where it takes me.

I probably shouldn't start another conversation with 'I saw some fairies and demons in my local park,' though. I can't always get as lucky as I did with Leverett.

I wander back to my seat and pick up my book.

'You've given me a lot to think about,' I say. 'Thank you for this.'

She smiles. 'Always a pleasure, Esta. Just ask if you have more questions.'

I'm tempted to leave it there, but I appreciate her opinion too much not to ask.

'I've been thinking about doing a photography project around this. I know I need to be careful, but I also feel like it's the right move. Do you think it could work?'

Is it my imagination or do her eyes turn dark for a moment?

'I don't think that's a good idea,' Kate says. 'If you approach them, that's your choice. If they decide to be open with you, that's theirs. But don't force them into the open against their will.'

I take a deep breath. 'That's what I'm worried about.' I bite my lip. This needs a lot of consideration to get right, but I can't shake the feeling that I should go ahead. Call it a gut feeling.

I've always got carried away when I was excited about something. It hasn't always worked out, like that time I was a child and decided it'd be fun to run down a steep hill. If my dad hadn't already been at the bottom and heard my mum shout, no one would have caught me, and I'd have run full speed through the fence and over the cliff. If I don't think this through before I start running, I'll throw myself into an abyss, and there won't be anyone waiting to catch me this time.

CHAPTER
NINE

My dreamscape looks bigger that night. Physically, nothing has changed, but now I sense the secrets lying beneath it all.

If Jung's theory about the collective unconscious is right, then we all carry our ancestors' knowledge and fears in us... and if that's true, there must be answers in my dreams since they are my unconscious made visual.

Lucid dreaming has always been something I just did. I've had a lot of fun with it, but I only attached the name to it when I read about other people doing it and saw myself in what they described. I never thought about how lucky I am to have all this at my fingertips. After today, I'm more grateful than ever. Reading books for research is great, but what if I could see a memory with my own eyes?

The only trouble is that dreams rarely make things obvious. They speak through symbolism more often than not, and I can just imagine that information from a few generations ago has become more confused, like a story passed down again and again. My own perceptions and knowledge might cloud it, too, which will make things harder.

That doesn't stop me from being excited to go exploring, though. Approaching strangers to talk about their magical origins is a terrible idea, but my dreams are perfectly safe. If I do run into a nightmare, Mischief can help me if needed, and I can always wake myself up if all else fails.

Kate told me to be cautiously open-minded, so that's what I'll do.

Mischief jumps onto my legs. 'You feel restless. Where are we going?'

I've been sitting at the base of the purple-leafed tree without moving a muscle, but she would know that my thoughts are racing since she's part of my mind.

'I don't know,' I say. 'I don't care. Anywhere—I want to go anywhere there are secrets.'

The last few days have opened my eyes to, well, everything. Meeting a vampire, Kate saying there's magic in everything… It's what I always wanted. Maybe my collective unconscious told me that this *is* what the world is really like—I didn't see it until now, but deep down I've always known. I just confused knowledge for wishing.

'That shouldn't be difficult,' Mischief purrs. 'Secrets are everywhere if you look close enough.'

And that's exactly what I intend to do—look at everything twice.

I start with my tree. I've always loved sitting here. It's been a source of comfort and relaxation. I've even touched the bark for strength before facing a fear. Still, it's always looked like a tree to me—a very lovely tree, but still just a tree. When I look at it now, I see the magic as golden rivulets flowing up the trunk into the leaves, which sparkle with life. Is this what Kate sees when she looks at plants? Is this what she meant earlier when she told me to look at my apple tree? If everyone saw this magic… I shake my head. We'd have chopped down even more trees to try and bottle it. It's probably for the best that I'm only seeing it here.

'Mischief?'

'Esta?'

'How do I tap into the collective unconscious?'

Because knowing it exists and actually… finding it? Going to it? It's not the same thing. I only know that in theory, it already exists as part of my unconscious, but it's not like there's a door for me to go through. But since it's part of my unconscious, Mischief will know.

Yet Mischief huffs at me and washes her face. 'I don't know.'

So much for that plan.

'Let's go to the caves,' I say. Something about ancient secrets hiding in dark underground spaces sits right with me. Maybe I'm romanticising it. Maybe it's my ancestors showing me the way. I won't know until I get there.

Mischief gives me puppy—well, kitty—eyes. 'But that's all the way over there.'

'Yup. And so is what I want. You can totally stay here if you want.'

She stretches—extra long for effect, I suspect—and shakes herself. 'No, let's go. I'm curious, too.'

I will myself to the caves, and the landscape changes. It's so much easier once I've been to a place or have somewhere specific I want to go. I couldn't have done this with the void lake since I had no idea where I was going or what I'd find. It wouldn't work with the collective unconscious because I don't have a place in mind for that, either, except that the caves feel right. I don't have the same internal pull I had with the lake, though, so really I'm just guessing.

'Show me...' I'm not sure how to phrase my request. What exactly do I want? I can't ask for one of my own memories, because as far as I know, no one I've ever met before Leverett is anything other than human. Maybe some part of my soul remembers something from another life, or maybe it's all indexed in some kind of cosmic archive.

We enter one of the caves—the opening is large, but I know I'll be squeezing through narrow gaps and jumping down holes before long—and my whole body tingles like it always does when I'm about to find something.

'Are we looking for anything specific?' Mischief asks.

'Not really,' I say. 'I just want to *see*.'

The ground falls away. I have a bizarre cartoon moment where I look at my feet, realise that I'm standing on a hole... and then fall because my self-preservation instinct knows that I need ground to stand on. I will myself to gently glide down the hole. It's tight. I can't see much around me, but when I stretch out my hands I feel smooth walls millimetres away from me. It's more like I'm in a tunnel. Blue and golden lights flash by; they remind me of distant stars.

Then I'm no longer falling or floating—it doesn't end smoothly or harshly as it would if I were really falling or floating. It just is, because dream logic. I stand inside a cave.

An underground lake expands before me and disappears into the cave's depths. Bright shades dance around the water, but I can't make out features. I think they look humanoid, but they're more like long lights with maybe wings coming out of their backs. Smaller shapes huddle by the water. There's nothing special about them, at least not in the same way as the dancing lights.

I sit and observe. I know with dream certainty that water fairies are getting to know their human neighbours who have come for water. There must be an entrance to this cave, but I don't see one. This could mean many things in the dream language of symbolism, but I don't want to make assumptions. The humans back away a little from the fairies, but they don't interact otherwise, just observe.

I've no idea what kind of fairy this is, and my dream instincts tell me their name is lost to time. They resemble will-o'-the-wisps in that they are made of light, but their shapes are closer to pixies—tiny humanoid creatures with wings, the shape most people think of when they picture fairies. Leverett did say there was a war. What if they were destroyed? What if they chose to hide even more than the others, and that's why I haven't seen any mentions of them? There are so many potential reasons. My instincts tell me that they no longer exist.

They are beautiful, little shapes of light flitting across the water almost like they're trying to impress the humans. Maybe their dance is a kind of offering. The humans wouldn't have known if this is their first meeting; they remain cautious and don't approach. Some back away farther.

The landscape changes, and I find myself inside a forest. Golden light falls through the green leaves. The nature magic in the air is so strong that it makes the sunshine glow brighter and tickles my skin. The air is alive here. A giggle escapes me.

'Esta—'

It's not just the air—this whole forest feels alive, both with magic and with pure joy. Part of me wants to dance, but no one wants to see that, even if it is just a dream.

'Be careful, Esta. Humans aren't used to magic this potent.'

I nod, but I'm not sure what Mischief expects me to do about it. This is just a dream, and I'm just exploring. What kind of explorer would I be if I didn't investigate?

'Look.'

I follow Mischief's gaze and find two men—two *naked* men—lying on leaves and foliage. Their clothes lay discarded on the side. Dream certainty tells me that it's the early nineteenth century, and they've been here for a hundred years. They don't look like they should be dead, though. Blissful smiles grace their lips. I don't imagine they'd be naked if they weren't comfortable, either.

I've heard stories of the fairy realm and all the warnings that come with it: Don't eat the food, don't drink the wine, don't go at all if you can help it. These two guys don't seem to have heard the same stories, or maybe they have and didn't care. Is it possible to wander into the fairy realm by accident? Is it possible to leave? By the smiles on their faces, I don't think they want to go anywhere, and the world they knew is gone. Would they even want to return if offered the chance?

I want to know what happens next, but the scenery changes

again. The smells of war hit me, and I gag.

I stand amongst bodies. No matter where I look, there are corpses. Many appear human—dream instincts know the difference, even when little more remains than bones and torn flesh—but there are many winged and fur-covered bodies, too. Some of the corpses are burned beyond any recognition. Others were torn apart by claws or fangs or maybe both. I spot a tall fairy near a heap of still-smouldering bodies. Someone ripped off his wings.

There's a strange sizzle in the air, like electricity, but I don't see the source. It feels awful and makes me want to run. Is this what dying magic feels like?

It's been years since I last had a nightmare. This is worse: Leverett told me about this, which means it really happened. People lived this, justified it. Leverett said the Veiled wanted peace, but all this death happened anyway. I don't blame them for hiding if it prevents a repeat. All this magic, all this beautiful variety, and we slaughtered each other.

This must have been so long ago, but is it possible that there's someone still alive today who remembers this? Is it possible that anyone alive today fought in this battle? Definitely no humans—if this were recent history, we'd know unless someone went to great effort to wipe every mention from the history books—but other people live much longer lives than we do. Vampires are said to be immortal, and I don't remember any stories about fairies dying of old age or being killed at all. The mutilated fairy by the burning bodies shows me how wrong I am.

'I don't want to see any more.'

But I look over the scene one last time. No one has remembered these people in so long. They deserve a little recognition. They deserve an apology, too, but there are no words that will make this right or better. Only the prevention of another war will. It doesn't matter how badly I want my photography project—if this is the price, it's not worth it.

Mischief looks at me, tail between her legs and ears pinned back. 'Yes, let's leave.'

I will us back to my purple-leafed tree and slide down the trunk. Gently, I run my hand through the yellow grass. I change it back to red; I need the comfort of familiarity right now.

'Did that satisfy your curiosity?' Mischief asks.

The words sound like an accusation, but she climbs onto my lap and hides her face in my arms. Neither of us wants to revisit that.

'It's not what I expected,' I say. 'Although, to be honest, I don't know what I thought I'd find. Not this. I'm not surprised they'd rather hide their whole lives.'

Mischief narrows her eyes at me. 'You're still thinking about doing that project, aren't you?'

My heart beats faster. 'No.'

'You're aware that you can't lie to me?'

I sigh. 'I am thinking about it, but not in the same way. I don't want to expose anyone. I just…' It makes sense in my head in a way that I can't put into words yet. 'What if I can bring both sides together? They want peace, and so do I. Not every human would want war.'

'And how will you do this project without exposing them?'

I shake my head. 'I don't know.' If it were obvious, I expect I'd have thought of it years ago. *Difficult* isn't the same as *impossible*, though.

'Remember what Leverett and Kate said,' Mischief said. 'They both think it's a terrible idea.'

I look up into the purple leaves and place my hand on the rough bark. 'I swear I won't endanger anyone. That's not what I want.'

'Then don't do the project.'

Mischief is part of me. In moments like this, she gives voice to my conscience.

'I won't,' I say. I don't add *at least not like I planned*. Mischief knows anyway.

CHAPTER
TEN

I wake up to the smell of rain. Petrichor is my second favourite smell, right after vellichor. There's something so relaxing and grounding about it, and after last night's dream, I need it. I open my curtains and take one more indulgent breath in before I close the window. It's cooled down a lot; I freeze too easily for this sudden change in temperature.

I try to wash the heaviness of that battle scene off me in the shower, but I can't shake the memory of that poor fairy and his bloody wings beside his body. I shiver under the hot water.

I can't go ahead with my project as I wanted, but that's fine. Projects change and evolve all the time. There has got to be some gentle way to draw attention to these people and foster peace and freedom without starting another war, but I can't for the life of me see what it is. I have been dwelling on it a lot, though. Maybe I should do something else for a day to take my mind off it. Chances are the solution will come to me while I do something unrelated.

I jump when there's a knock on the bathroom door. If I'm this on edge about it, I definitely need a break. I peek around the shower curtain, and the door opens a sliver.

'Morning!' Bonnie sticks her head into the bathroom. 'I'm starving. Do you want pancakes or fry-up?'

As good as sausages, beans, and eggs sound right now, I'll never turn down pancakes. Then again, I've often thought of a fry-up as a good breakfast to reset—something to have after reaching an achievement to launch me into the next step—and that sounds good, too.

Pancakes, though.

'Murder those pancakes with chocolate,' I say.

Bonnie grins. 'Gladly!'

By the time I'm done showering and getting into pjs—I need the comfort after what I saw last night—the whole house smells like sweet batter.

Lady greets me when I enter the kitchen just as Bonnie slides another pancake onto a plate. There's a tiny bit of batter left in the bowl—one more pancake and breakfast will be served.

'Did you hear the thunder last night?' Bonnie asks.

She pours the cold batter into the hot frying pan, and we close our eyes in sizzle-appreciation. There's no sound homier than anything frying in melted butter, or just anything frying full stop. It sounds like satisfaction and noms.

The sound fades; I open my eyes again.

'No, I had no idea. Was it that bad?'

She nods. 'Have a look outside.'

I look out the window and gasp. A most terrible storm has ravaged the south of England—our empty watering can has fallen over.

'No! I can't believe I missed the apocalypse!' I laugh. 'I was out as soon as my head hit the pillow.'

I don't see any mugs on the table, so I fill the kettle for Bonnie's coffee and my and Lady's tea. My stomach rumbles when my sister flips the pancake and it sizzles again.

If I don't tell anyone else what I've learned, I want to tell her. Maybe she'll have an answer I haven't considered.

But she doesn't believe in the paranormal quite like I do, so I don't know what she'll make of it. Maybe that's good, though. She won't be biased.

Bonnie puts the plates with three pancakes each onto the table and slides over the chocolate spread.

'I've murdered them, as requested, but here's more if it's not enough.'

'Thank you for breakfast.' I bite my lip. 'Can I get your opinion on something?'

She nods. 'Of course. Thank you for the coffee!'

I take a big sip of tea for clarity and to hide my nose from her coffee's stench. I've never been a fan of the taste or the smell, but she inhales it like it's bliss.

'I've thought of a new photography project'—her eyes sparkle at the idea—'but I don't know if I should do it.'

Her forehead creases. 'Why not?'

I drink some more tea to buy time. 'I want to base it on the paranormal. Remember that project I did at uni, the surrealism one?'

I took black-and-white pictures of myself with exposures of a few seconds. I moved in every picture so I looked like a ghost in the prints. Since I took them with a film camera, the overall effect was even spookier.

'Yes!' Bonnie says between mouthfuls. 'I loved that one.'

'It'll be like that, but instead of focussing on ghosts, I'll focus on elves'—her eyes sparkle brighter still—'mermaids, fairies, and so on.'

'That's a great idea! Why do you think it's not?'

Bring it on, moment of truth.

'Because they might not appreciate it, and I don't know what the best way to go about it is.'

I'm not saying her eyes lose their sparkle, but she's definitely more confused than she was a moment ago.

'What do you mean?'

'I saw some in the park and on the high street. That's where the idea comes from.'

She stops eating. 'Wait, what? You saw real mermaids?'

'No, of course not. We're nowhere near the water.' I hoped that she would laugh, but she just looks more confused. 'I saw fairies, though, and some others.'

She sits back like it'll help her process this. 'Like, real fairies?'

'I know it sounds ridiculous, but I swear I did! I talked to Kate, and she knows about them, too. And I—'

I nearly blurted out Leverett's name. Fortunately, I stop myself before it slips out. It's not my secret to tell. Leverett trusted me with it, but does he trust me to tell other people? If Bonnie finds out, it'll have to come from him.

So instead, I keep it vague. 'And I met a vampire.'

Her eyes go wide. 'A real one? How do you know?'

'I saw his fangs.'

'They could be plastic.'

I nod. Given how easily I get carried away when I'm excited, it's a good thing that she questions things more. She keeps me grounded.

'They could, *but* I also saw him turn into fog and fly up the stairs.'

'And were you properly hydrated at the time?'

I laugh and playfully punch her arm. 'I was!' I kinda wasn't, but that's not the point. 'I'm telling you, I met a vampire, and I saw fairies, probably a werewolf, maybe angels—'

'Whoa, hold up.'

I dig into my pancakes while she swirls her coffee around. She needs a moment, and I can't argue with that. It *is* a lot.

'If they're running around the park,' she says slowly, 'how haven't I seen any? I'm there all the time.'

I explain the whole dream-lake thing until she's all caught up.

'Look,' she says, 'it's not that I don't believe you, but it's hard to judge this without seeing it. If they're worried about a war or something, I get why they're hiding, but...' She pouts. 'And I'm not dangerous or anything, I wouldn't want a war, either. They can totally show themselves to me.'

I laugh, but it gives me an idea.

'Maybe they would,' I say. 'The vampire said that some people need charms or spells to appear human, but he just grew his fangs and turned into fog in front of me. Maybe he could show you, too.'

Her eyes start to shine again. 'You think he would?'

I shrug. 'I don't know, but I won't put him on the spot. I'll ask first, okay?'

She nods. 'That seems fair.'

In my head, we're already the best group ever—me, Bonnie, my vampire friend, and my witch neighbour. There's room for Lady, too. I meant what I said, though—I won't put Leverett on the spot. He already might not like that I said anything to Bonnie at all, but I didn't give her a name or his address, so it's not like she knows who he is. If he doesn't want to show her, he can say no.

I giggle and feel like a little girl with the juiciest secret, only I'm not five and it seems disrespectful to call their survival struggle *juicy*.

'I'll ask next time I see him. But if he says no… Maybe it'd be okay to get a picture of a fairy just to show you? People take photos in the park all the time. I'd hardly stand out.'

Although, most of those people take pictures of their children, and I don't have one of those. That's if the photos would come out at all—any of the Veiled might just look like a regular human on camera. What determines if a fairy shows up in a photo as fae or as human? The media is full of pictures. We once did a workshop at uni where we had to take photos of the high street, and not one of those pictures showed anything other than humans. Maybe it's a permission thing. Maybe the glamour would need to come off first. If that's the case, my project won't go anywhere anyway, and Leverett is my only chance at proving to Bonnie that I'm not losing my mind.

'Sounds exciting'—Bonnie stands and picks up her plate—'but I need to go. I ended up talking to the instructor and she offered to meet me for a chat today.'

My mind goes blank. 'Instructor?'

She downs the rest of her coffee. 'The diving instructor. I went diving yesterday.'

My mouth falls open. I got so excited about my own discoveries that I completely forgot to ask.

'I'm sorry, I should have remembered. How was it? Who's this instructor?'

She smiles, and I know she's not angry. 'It was awesome. We didn't go too far out since there were lots of first-time divers and our dogs were there, but I asked about going farther and she offered to discuss it.'

'Sounds like a sales pitch.'

It's Bonnie's turn to punch my arm. Unlike me, who wasn't blessed with muscles, her karate-trained arms hit a lot harder.

'I suppose it kind of is,' Bonnie says. 'But I'd still love to go if she's got something. Just for fun, you know? No uni report attached to it.'

I nod, but I can't remember the last time I took pictures just for fun. It's always been about the next project, about finding that big idea.

Maybe that's why I've been struggling. I've forgotten how to enjoy it.

'That sounds fun,' I say. 'Hope it goes well.'

I wait until she's off to meet the instructor, and then I'm off, too. I've got some new questions I need answers to.

When I arrive at the bookshop, Leverett is helping a customer. I've got so used to this shop being empty that I'm taken aback for a second, but I'm happy that I'm not the only one here. It'd be a shame if he had to pack up again because his sole returning customer only ever comes by for a chat. I smile at him and browse until he's done.

I merely pretend to read the spines, though. Really, I wish the guy would buy the book already. It's selfish of me, but I want answers too badly to just open books at random in peace. I turn around when I hear the bell. The customer is gone, and Leverett comes over.

'I'm glad I didn't scare you away,' he says.

I laugh. 'Please, it takes more than that to scare me.'

I kinda wish I hadn't said that. I'm not a fan of horror movies and don't want him getting any ideas.

'I mean, you were just being you,' I say. 'That doesn't scare me.'

He slightly cocks his head to the side. 'Maybe it should.'

A shiver runs down my back. He *is* a predator—if he wanted to, he could probably kill me and hide my body so no one would ever find me. But I don't believe that he would, so really there's nothing to worry about.

Still, after everything I've learned about him lately, his stare is a little too intense. I gulp before I keep talking.

'I have some more questions, if that's alright?'

He glances towards the door and nods. 'I can take an early break.'

Bonnie and I were up late and she took another hour before she left, so it's nearly lunch time. The high street is filling up; it wouldn't surprise me if a lot of customers come in on their breaks.

'Are you sure?' I ask. 'I'd hate for you to miss out on a few sales because of me.'

He smiles. 'It's fine. He wasn't a customer but an old friend.'

I look towards the door like he's still there, like I'd study every detail on his face if he were. 'He's a vampire, too?'

Leverett laughs. 'We are everywhere.'

I wonder how true that statement is. From what he said last time, humans outnumber everyone else, so he probably means the collective *we* rather than vampires alone. Given how many wings, tails and whatnot I've seen just on brief walks, it's clear he isn't kidding.

He walks to the door and turns the sign around. 'Would you like a tea?'

I smile. 'Thank you, I'd love one. Are you sure it's okay to just close?'

I feel like I've complicated things for him by coming over. Would he still have taken a break if I hadn't come?

I follow him into the back.

'I'm the only employee here,' Leverett says. 'Am I not entitled to a lunch break?'

I nod, feeling a little less guilty. 'My mum always said I get grumpy when I don't eat, so I wouldn't keep you from yours.' I jump on the easy opening. 'Do you eat, though?'

He turns around and raises an eyebrow. 'You mean, do I drink blood?'

I swallow. 'Yes, but... Sorry, that's probably a rude question.'

'Not at all.' He gestures to the stairs. 'Would you like to come up? I haven't made it very homey, but it's nicer than these boxes.'

My heart skips a beat. This feels personal, but one glance around the storage room and I can't deny that I'd prefer a chair. A small voice at the back of my mind tells me that this is how I'll die, but I ignore it. If he wanted to kill me, he's had plenty of chances.

'I...' I don't want to intrude on his personal space—we haven't known each other that long, even if it feels longer in a good way—but he wouldn't have offered if he didn't mean it. 'Thank you.'

He turns into fog and flies up the stairs. I feel so last year walking like some boring hu— Oh, right.

He wasn't joking when he said that he hasn't decorated. The room is sparse. A door at the top of the stairs keeps it private. It was shut when he invited me up, but he must have flown through the keyhole or under the gap, because it opens shortly after he disappears. Inside is a large room which spans the entire shop floor. There's a sofa, an armchair, and a dusty coffee table. Various herbs are growing in pots along the windows. I recognise chamomile, peppermint, and sage—the source of his homegrown tea. Next to the stairs and separated by a wall is a small kitchen. It's an open floor plan, so I can watch him make tea if I want to. There's one door to the right and one to the left, I'm assuming to a bathroom and a bedroom. I won't go to check, though, or I really would be intruding.

'Please,' he says from the kitchenette, 'make yourself comfortable.'

The smell of cinnamon begins to fill the space, and I breathe deep.

Does he use the armchair or the sofa when he's alone? I don't want to claim "his" seat. I decide to wait and join him in the small kitchen.

'Can I do anything?'

He shakes his head. 'It would be awfully rude of me to invite you into my lair and then make you prepare the teas.'

I laugh again. 'You call this a lair? Where are the catacombs and coffins?'

He gives me a curious look as he strains the leaves. 'I see you've been to many vampire lairs. And here I thought this was special.'

I smirk and accept my tea. 'Thank you.' I hold my nose to the rim and inhale, then curse when it burns my nostrils.

'Careful,' he says, 'it's hot.'

I want to punch his arm like I punched Bonnie's earlier, but maybe we aren't *that* close just yet, no matter how easy this feels.

He sits in the armchair, so I get comfy on the sofa.

'To answer your earlier question,' he says, 'I have the same tea as you, but yes, vampires do drink blood. I simply choose not to.'

I blow on my tea to cool it and sip. 'Not at all? Isn't that bad for you?'

My mum is right: I definitely get cranky when I don't eat dinner.

'It weakens and ages us,' he says. 'It's hard at first. New vampires struggle with control, but it's not easy for experienced ones, either. It's similar to if you were to give up food, only your body shuts down much faster than mine.'

I pale. Does he mean—

'You'll die?'

'Not for a good few hundred years yet.'

This is not the direction I thought this conversation would go.

'Then why…' It's really none of my business. By the time it happens, I'll have been dead for a few centuries, but I still don't like the idea of him, or anyone, slowly starving himself. I'm not an idiot—I know everyone dies—but he has a choice. One that's in tune with his nature. 'Sorry. You don't need to answer that.'

'It's fine. Mostly, it's courtesy—your blood belongs to you, not me. A very long time ago, we simply took. Had we continued that way, humanity would be extinct by now, which is why all-out hunts are frowned upon and strictly regulated. Some vampires still prefer to take what they want, but it's become an outdated view.'

'So you're making up for the past by slowly killing yourself?'

I *really* wish I hadn't said that.

'Does it bother you?' he asks.

I have no answer.

'I will outlive you by several centuries.'

It's his decision. He seems at peace with it. And yet… Yes. It bothers me.

'There isn't anything you want to stay alive for?' I ask.

He doesn't look offended, but his usual smile is gone and it makes my heart ache.

'I have lived a long time. Longer, perhaps, than humans can

comprehend. I don't mean to patronise you; I simply mean that to imagine living for several hundred years and to actually live that long are two very different things. I have seen much, but I have also lost much. Vampires are much like werewolves in that we are loyal to those we love, be it friends or family or lovers. We don't move on easily when we commit.'

'I'm sorry,' I say. 'I shouldn't have asked. What you do with your long life is up to you. It's certainly not up to me.'

He's right, I can't imagine living that long. I can barely remember what I did last week, so the thought of living for a few hundred years is overwhelming. How would I cope if I watched everyone I love die or move on without me? Maybe I see his point.

'But it does upset you.' He doesn't sound angry or insulted, just curious. 'May I ask why?'

'Because I...' I'm not sure how to answer. Why *does* it bother me so much? 'You're a good man, Leverett, at least I think you are. I hate the idea that you have nothing you want to live for. That there's no one who makes you want to stay. You deserve better.'

And the smile is back. My heart jumps a little.

'I thank you for your concern, but I've made my peace with it.'

From anyone else, it might have sounded sarcastic, but it sounds genuine from his lips.

'Would you like another tea?'

I nod and watch him as he puts the kettle on again. Leverett looks tired; I instinctively blame the lack of blood. It could be any number of reasons, but that's what comes to mind. His lips are dry, his eyes a little bloodshot. He looks like he needs a nap followed by a holiday. How many friends do vampires have? Are centuries-long friendships common? Maybe that's why he's so open with me—he may be as glad to have someone to talk to as I am.

Desperate to change the subject, I say, 'Don't you need to get back to the shop? I don't want to keep you from paying customers.'

His eyes linger on mine a moment. 'It's really no problem. I could close this shop for a year or two and money still wouldn't be an issue.'

I raise my eyebrows. 'Why would you choose such a small place if you have that kind of money?' I bite my lip. 'Sorry. That's none of my business, either.'

He chuckles as he hands me the hot tea. Its warmth spreads through my hands—not ideal since the weather is warming up again.

'I prefer smaller places,' he says. 'Some vampires prefer to live in luxury, but I've never had the patience for it. Smaller places feel more like home, especially when I can fill them with vellichor and herbs.'

I sigh into my tea. It's hard to argue with logic.

'I know we weren't serious when we called this my lair, but during the witch hunts, I stayed in catacombs for a while. Humans usually avoid those, so it was peaceful.'

I nearly choke on my tea from laughter. 'You cliché.'

'You would have liked it,' he says. 'I lit a few candles for atmosphere, and I started my book collection around that time, too. On rainy days you didn't have to venture outside to smell the petrichor.'

I give him a sceptical look. 'Do you even need candles? Or is the seeing-in-the-dark thing a lie, too?'

'No, I see perfectly fine without them. I found their light comforting, however. It wasn't a good time to be different.'

I desperately want to ask how old he is, but even socially awkward me knows that's rude. I'm grateful it doesn't just slip out for once—I guess even my excitement has some decency.

'Well, it sounds downright romantic.'

I... don't know where that came from. *People were hanged and drowned, Esta.*

'I mean, because of the candles. Not because of the times.'

Leverett nods, and I drown whatever might have come out next in the tea— No, not *drown*. That's disrespectful, too, since he mentioned—

I swallow a big mouthful of tea. I'll just shut up now.

'Sorry,' I say. 'It's been a strange few days.'

'Would you like to sit again?'

I wasn't even aware that I was still standing. I mean, yes, I know I'm not sitting down, but it wasn't a conscious decision to stay on my feet. I should have noticed it sooner since there isn't that much space in the kitchen and he's standing close to me in this small space. If we'd known each other for longer, I'd hug him after everything he said, to try to warm him. Would he feel cold? I resist the urge to reach out in the name of research.

'Sure,' I say. 'There was something else I meant to ask you.'

I wait until he sits, too. He's been walking since we got up here—no more of the flashy fog stuff.

'I see you're done showing off.'

'Did I make you uncomfortable?'

I shake my head. 'No, not at all. I just...'

I've no idea where I was going with that, so I leave it before I start the next awkward conversation I have zero business asking about.

'In truth, it was a test,' he says. 'I apologise. I thought you might explain my fangs away, but my turning into fog would be harder to rationalise. I wanted to see your reaction.'

I huff into my tea. 'And did I pass?'

He nods and smiles. 'You did.'

I hide my face in my tea. I've never been great in social situations, but I'm not sure why I'm *this* awkward now.

'I don't suppose that was your question?' Leverett asks.

How did I forget? *Focus, Esta.*

'Since you mentioned explaining away fangs...' I hope he won't be angry that I sort of told Bonnie. 'I told my sister about my photography idea—we share everything. She hasn't seen what I've seen, though. She said it could just have been plastic teeth. I didn't tell her who you are, I just said I met a vampire.'

He's quiet for a moment as he takes a long sip.

'You don't want to touch my teeth, do you?'

I choke on my tea again. If this keeps happening, being around Leverett will become a health hazard.

'No!' I laugh through the coughs. 'Bloody hell, Leverett, have people asked to do that?'

He chuckles at my teary cough-laugh. 'No, but I wasn't sure where you were going.'

I take two deep breaths to make sure the tea is no longer burning my throat. 'I was wondering if she could meet you. I didn't want to tell her about you in case you weren't okay with it, but I know she'll have a hard time believing me if she doesn't see proof.' That came out all wrong. 'I don't mean you'd be some kind of test subject.'

He looks at me like that didn't occur to him for one second.

'Thank you for not giving my identity away at the earliest opportunity,' he says.

Now I feel terrible for asking.

'It might not sound like much,' he says, 'but it means a lot. If you trust her and are sure that she can keep it quiet, then I'll trust you.'

'I trust her with my life,' I say. A bit dramatic maybe, but it's true, and I need him to know I'm serious.

He nods. 'I leave the details up to you, but allow me to make it clear that this is an exception.'

'Oh, absolutely. We're not about to go around the neighbourhood with fliers or pitchforks.' Shit, that's probably a sore subject. 'We won't tell anyone. I promise.'

He stands and holds out his hand for my cup.

'Then consider me assured.'

I pass him the mug, his finger brushes my knuckles…

And I realise why I've been so awkward.

Stupid me is falling in love with a vampire.

CHAPTER ELEVEN

I've always been drawn to graveyards. There's a quiet peace about them, a serene hush I've always adored. When I was younger, I thought that dark magics happened in graveyards, and since I desperately wanted all kinds of magic to be real, I loved graveyards for the possibility. As I grew older, I imagined that ghosts came out at night and got together to talk, make new ghost friends, and otherwise kill time. I smile to myself. *Kill time*—it's funny 'cause they're dead.

No one lies buried in my dream graveyard. These graves are here simply because I want them to be. I've wondered a few times if all the fears I've faced and defeated over the years are buried here, or perhaps versions of the Esta I used to be, but as far as I can tell, it's only ever been me and Mischief and that wonderful silence.

Tonight, I hoped for some of that quiet peace, but it's not enough to make sense of my confusion. I place my hand on a cool tombstone, but it doesn't ground me. I feel strangely watched, like I'm not the only one here. I look down and Mischief squints up at me from the grey grass; muting the colours feels right here.

She straightens like she's putting on her professional parent hat. 'Do you want to talk about it?'

'No.' I sigh. 'I don't know.'

'I mean, a vampire, Esta. Really?'

I frown at her. Not everyone has the chance to reason through something with their own unconscious. Maybe I should take the chance—in fact, I most definitely should. Mischief is giving me attitude, but only because I'm giving myself attitude. If I weren't confused about how on earth I developed feelings for Leverett, she wouldn't be, either.

'Yes, I'm aware,' I say.

But I don't *understand*. When did this happen? While Leverett was talking about how he's slowly starving himself? When he mentioned the witch hunts he had to hide from? I slam my fist into the tree trunk and immediately stroke over it in apology afterwards. It's not the tree's fault. The tree has been nothing but good to me and deserves better.

I sit down at the roots, and Mischief jumps onto my lap.

'Is this why we're in a graveyard?' Mischief asks. 'Is he here?'

I frown at her and roll my eyes. 'No, that's not why we're in a graveyard.' Or is it? Damn, I don't know anymore. Leverett did mention that he stayed in some catacombs for a while. Is that why my mind decided this was the right place? I pout at myself, at my mind, Mischief, this whole situation, and say, 'We're here because it's relaxing.'

'Uh-huh. Do you think he's handsome?'

I never thought I'd have this kind of talk with my dream guide, but why not? If it saves me the brain power while I'm awake…

'Yes.'

My parents would tell me that he's too old for me, but his age seems irrelevant since he's a vampire—he was never going to be my age, was he? Leverett said something about new vampires struggling to control themselves; I can just imagine what a pain a thirty-year-old vampire might be. A busy high street full of people on their periods comes to mind. Now there's a nightmare no one wants.

I've never been in a long-term relationship with anyone much older than me, but my few short-term relationships with guys my age were annoying and didn't last for a reason. Usually, that reason was clubbing and them being too immature for my patience. I don't have that with Leverett. Our conversations are easy. I can open up to him.

I blush at the thought of me opening myself to him. Of his hands stroking up my legs, slipping into my underwear. Of the gleam in his eyes when he draws the first soft moan from me.

Oh, hell. How am I ever supposed to set foot in that shop again?

'Emotional connections are important,' Mischief says. 'It's not a small thing that you can really talk to him.'

I'm grateful that she doesn't comment on where else my mind went for a second.

'I can be myself when I talk to him. I don't often have that.'

'So there's your answer.'

My forehead wrinkles. 'There is?'

'You probably slowly developed feelings for him over your conversations.' She blinks. 'And his smile, right?'

I blush again. I can see how his smile may have been my undoing.

I liked the guys I dated before, but my feelings for them never hit me like this—hard and fast and—

I blush more fiercely. My next visit to his shop will be interesting. Or a nightmare. Or an interesting nightmare.

Maybe he has a website I can order from.

My mum always said that you don't choose who you fall in love with. It happens whether you like it or not. It's too early to call this *love*, but I can't pretend that I'm not developing feelings, either. I guess I'll see how much of a fool I make of myself next time I see him.

Mischief paws at my face to bring my attention back to her. 'Do you think he noticed the change in your heartbeat when he brushed against your hand?'

I swear my whole dreamscape stands still.

'What do you mean.'

It's not a question, because I know exactly what she means. I just don't want to consider it, and I really don't want Mischief spelling it out.

'Well,' she says anyway, 'vampires are natural hunters with extra sharp senses, right? He probably noticed that your heart beat faster when you realised that you *lurve*—'

I give her a mortified glare, and Mischief shuts up. She giggles, though. I'm not convinced that's better. Having discussions with your unconscious is interesting and all until it starts to tease you.

She's probably right, though.

I can never go back to that bookshop.

I sigh and stand. Mischief jumps off my legs in the last second and gives me a scandalised look.

'Let's talk about something else,' I say. 'Does this'—I look around the meadow—'feel off to you?'

Mischief nods. 'I thought it was your powerful feelings for Leverett, but—' She stops when I shoot her another look. 'Sorry. I won't mention it again, but I thought that was why. Do you feel watched?'

I thought it was because Mischief was judging me. She's definitely still doing that, but I no longer think that's the reason. This feeling is darker, almost like a nightmare, but…

Bigger.

What's worse than a nightmare?

I steel myself. I've faced nightmares before; I'll deal with whatever this is, too. If it doesn't go well, I'll just wake up. It'll be fine.

It's been a while since I was nervous in a dream. The uncomfortable sense that I'm not entirely in control worms its way into my mind, and I can't shake it despite knowing that I'm the only one who *can* be in control. The dreamer is always more powerful in their own mind—that's Dream 101.

'Are you ready?' Mischief asks.

I don't know, and I don't like it. What can be so bad that it has me this unsure?

I nod, mostly to steady myself. 'Come out.'

I let my voice echo across the meadow. Whatever this nightmare is, it'll hear me anyway unless it's a fear of not being heard, which I don't think I have, but it's also partly to assert dominance. This thing thinks it can scare me in my own dreams? I don't bloody think so.

I am scared, though. And that worries me more than anything.

Everything goes black—not desaturated but *black*, like something has pulled a sheet over everything or thrown me into a room with black walls, only I don't see any corners or a door. It reminds me of the void lake, but this darkness is shapeless. There are no stars glittering in its depths.

And it's *empty*. I don't even see Mischief anywhere.

'What are you?'

Often, the best way to conquer your nightmares is to ask them why they scare you. I have a feeling it won't work here, though. My gut has never been this unhappy.

Out of the shadows, a… *creature* rises. It's a twisted thing, dressed in rags and covered in twigs and strings. Its movements are jerky, like something breaks and realigns with every step. If I saw this thing coming at me in a forest, I'd be too petrified to run.

And then it's right in front of me, close enough that I'm aware of the absence of breath. This close, I should feel it on my face, but there's nothing. I don't know if this means that it doesn't breathe or that there's nothing inside it.

A gasp escapes me and my limbs shake. I don't run, though. If you run from a nightmare, it'll chase you, and then you've already lost. I do not want this thing to come after me.

'Stop,' it rasps, and then I smell it after all—a strange combination of all the bad things in the world, like the battlefield I saw last time, gone-off lemons, and licorice.

I gulp. 'Stop what?'

'Do not expose us.'

He must mean my photography project. I've been so focussed on fairies and angels that something as twisted as this never even crossed my mind.

'What nightmare are you? Which fear do you represent?'

'I'm no nightmare,' it says, 'but I catch them. I will catch you, if you continue.'

I don't understand. Dreamcatchers catch, well, dreams, but they're pretty things I hang over my bed. This thing is nothing like it. My eyes flit to the twigs and strings sticking out from under its rags, and I reassess.

I will myself to stand straight and remind myself where I am. This is *my* dream. It can't hurt me if I don't let it. Leverett's and Kate's warnings to not do the photography project got to me more than I realised, that's all.

'No,' I say. 'You have no power over me here. If you represent my project, you're tied to my creativity.' I hope. 'You know my intentions.'

'Your intentions won't matter when we start to die.'

Dead bodies litter the ground around us. My parents. My cousins. Bonnie. Kate and Leverett. Even Lady.

I shake my head. I'm ready to wake up now, but nothing's happening. My heart begins to race. I've never been trapped in my own dreams before.

'I don't want you to d-die, either. I want to help you.'

I hate how desperate I sound, but not being in control is getting to me. How long will this thing keep me here? What happens if I simply don't wake up?

The creature raises a hand from under the twigs. It's gripped around Mischief's throat. She's thrashing and trying to claw at him, but he doesn't care.

A sob escapes me. My vision blurs. Nothing can hurt me or Mischief in here. This shouldn't be possible.

'Let her go.' I choke on the words.

'Do not expose us.'

I don't care about the project anymore. I care about my spirit cat.

'Don't—' I reach out, but in the same breath, the creature is farther away from me. Just out of reach. I instinctively know that I won't reach it.

'Do not expose us.'

'Let her go.' My lip quivers. '*Please.*'

I've never begged in my dreams before; I hate how small it makes me feel. Who the shit does it think it is, coming into my dream and threatening my spirit cat? Who does it think it is, trapping me here and taking my control away? I don't want to do what it says; I don't negotiate with terrorists.

But then there's a snap, and it throws Mischief's still body to my feet. She disappears in a huff of fog, blown away like brittle leaves in autumn, and there's this odd numb feeling somewhere at the back of my mind where she used to be.

I'm too stunned to react. I can't wrap my head around it. Mischief is gone. Killed by something in my dream. She was supposed to be safe here. None of this is meant to be possible.

'Do not expose us.'

It's been years since I woke up screaming and crying. I'm sobbing so hard that I can't get a word out to explain what happened when Bonnie rushes into my room and asks me what's wrong.

No nightmare has ever threatened me like this before, but the message is clear:

This creature, this Dreamcatcher, controls my dreams better than I do, and if I don't do what he demands, he'll snap me next.

CHAPTER
TWELVE

The following morning, I ghost through the house in my pjs and wrapped in a blanket. It's a comforting fort made of pillows and... and... Damn it, I can't think. I just know I need it.

It took a while, but once Bonnie calmed me down enough to talk, I explained what happened. I cried again when I got to the part about Mischief and that awful sound her neck made.

I have no idea what it means beyond the obvious warning. Maybe that's all it is. But what if the Dreamcatcher comes back? What if that's my dreamscape now? In theory, as long as I heed his threat he won't return, but I'm not so sure. What even was that thing? I thought I knew everything that happened in my unconscious—or sort of, anyway—but that monster doesn't belong in my head. That's not possible, though. Is it? Can something invade my dreams from the outside?

I shiver and hug the blanket tighter around myself. Whatever he is, it's clear to me that he has his own fears and motivations, so I no longer feel right referring to him as an *it*.

Although, I don't find the thought that he's a real person with sound reasoning reassuring either.

Once she got me comfortable on the sofa with a strong tea, Bonnie went next door and asked Kate to come over. Kate, in her eternal wisdom, figured Leverett's knowledge might prove useful and invited him over, too. Since neither Kate nor Bonnie know how the very idea of Leverett in my house makes me feel, they don't know how infuriatingly awkward I now am on top of being scared witless. Kate is right, though. She's visited his shop often enough to know that Leverett has a good understanding of all things paranormal. Their combined efforts are reassuring. We'll make sense of this together.

Because, scared as I am, I have no intention of just giving this monster what he wants. No one waltzes into my dreams, ki—*hurts* my spirit cat, and gets to make demands. I don't know what we'll do, but I'm positive that we'll figure something out.

Kate makes herself comfortable in our lounge on the spare sofa we rarely use. Bonnie and I tend to share one, but we thought having another would be good for when we have guests over, which never happens. Today, it finally comes in handy.

Leverett looks more reserved. Our eyes meet when he walks in and stands by the fireplace. I smile the most awkward smile in history and hide my blush in my blanket. Hopefully, he'll figure my cheeks are flushed because I've been sobbing, which is oddly preferable. My heart spiked when our eyes met, though; he probably heard it, which is just so fun. He'll probably figure I've been through a lot and am scared. I won't consider that he might remember how my heart jumped when he brushed against my hand, that he'll easily put two and two together. Totally not even thinking about that.

Bonnie settles next to me. I pull the blanket tighter around me for comfort but sit straighter. The least I can do with so many guests in our home is try to make myself look presentable. If I'd known that Leverett would be here, I'd at least have washed; I must smell of sleep and warm bed. I haven't even brushed my hair. I don't mind looking a mess in front of Kate—I often do when we chat over tea in the mornings—but Leverett... It shouldn't matter, but I'm not socially confident enough for this added pressure.

'Bonnie said you had a nightmare,' Kate says, 'but I see it's worse than that. Tell me what happened.'

Leverett is quiet, and my brain is trying to over-analyse why. Maybe he thinks I look a mess, which I do. Or maybe he wonders why on earth he was asked to come here, which wasn't my idea.

Or maybe, Esta, he's letting Kate take the lead because she's your neighbour and knows you better than he does. Get your shit together.

I tell them everything I remember, which is too much and probably not enough at the same time. Now that I've been awake for a bit and the tea is kicking in, my fear is melting a little and turning into caffeine, but the details still shake me to my core. Mischief on the ground, discarded like an old, unwanted toy. That awful *snap*.

I shiver.

'He said something about catching dreams, but he's not like

any dreamcatcher I've ever seen.'

I don't know what else to call him, though, so Dreamcatcher it is until he introduces himself.

There's a regular dreamcatcher over my bed right now. I've had one ever since my grandma gifted me my first one as a child. It's always been an object, not a monster. That it could be some evil beast defies all logic of what a dreamcatcher is supposed to be. Although…

Dreamcatchers are meant to catch nightmares. I never thought about what they do with them. Maybe the creature I met last night is the twisted result.

Kate frowns. 'I've never heard of such a being.' She looks to Leverett. 'Have you?'

He shakes his head. 'No, but…' He shifts to walk over to me but stops himself and stays at the fireplace. 'There's bound to be some mention in one of my books. I'll find it.'

I nod. If he says he'll find an answer, I believe him.

'Did he mention anything else?' Kate asks. 'Someone else?'

I shake my head. 'Not that I remember.' My forehead wrinkles. 'You don't think there's more than one, do you?' My heart drops at the thought of a whole army of those things.

Kate hesitates. 'I think we would do well to be cautious. If nothing else, his warning was clear.'

I grip my blanket. 'He hurt my cat.' I hope she's okay. It didn't sound good, but she's not a physical cat, she's made from ideas. 'It wasn't a warning, it was a threat.' I want to go so far as to say that it was a declaration of war, but that's just my emotions getting the better of me. Given that a war is the very thing I want to avoid, saying it out loud seems like a bad idea since the Dreamcatcher seems to know my plans.

'Be that as it may,' Kate says, 'I advise against ignoring him.'

I grit my teeth. 'He doesn't get to make demands of me.'

I'm scared, but this monster doesn't know me. Isn't it possible that he assumes the worst and acted without knowing my intentions? He said he knows what I want to do, but none of us have ever heard of him before. Maybe he misunderstood. Maybe he acted out of fear.

'Do either of you know of something that can cause nightmares like this?' Bonnie asks.

'Nothing like this,' Leverett says. 'I've heard of several creatures that can cause nightmares, but none who work like this one did.'

Kate nods. 'As far as I know, none enter your dreams and threaten you in person. It's unusual.'

'There must be something,' I say. 'I can't be the first person this has happened to.'

'Perhaps not,' Kate says, 'but not many have the same talent for lucid dreaming you do. Of those who do, not many threaten the balance the Veiled community has so carefully built.'

I want to argue that I'm not threatening anything—I haven't taken a single picture—but my eyes flick to Bonnie instead. She's gone still next to me.

'You mean…' She glances at me. 'Esta said she saw fairies. There's an actual supernatural community?'

I'm amazed that Kate slipped up, or maybe she thought I've told Bonnie by now. Whatever her motivations, it doesn't matter; I'm glad that Bonnie hears it from someone else. I glance at Leverett and blush again when he looks at me, too. This is ridiculous. *Get a grip, Esta.* I can't go red every time we look at each other.

Kate smiles at her. 'You've known for years that I'm a witch, haven't you?'

Bonnie shrugs. 'Yes, but you grow herbs and things like that. I don't think of you as superna—Veiled.' It's her turn to blush. 'I mean, I don't think of you as glowing or having wings or anything like that.'

Kate laughs. 'While my talents may be perfectly ordinary and teachable to anyone, many would still see me as unnatural, don't you think?'

'I don't—' Bonnie looks to me for help, and I smile. We're both socially awkward in similar ways. 'Sorry. So, the vampire you mentioned…'

I won't look at Leverett if he doesn't want to give himself away right now—not just to Bonnie but also to Kate—but I don't have to.

He inclines his head. 'Nice to meet you.'

By the lack of reaction on Kate's part, I've a feeling she already knew. Figures.

Bonnie pales a little but nods. 'And you.'

'So,' I say, 'what do we do from here? Is there anything I can do so I can sleep tonight?'

I'm embarrassed to admit it, but I'm scared to fall asleep. What if the Dreamcatcher is there tonight and every night from now on? Maybe he won't say anything. Maybe he'll just watch me from the shadows. I don't want to feel watched by the monster that hurt Mischief every night for the rest of my life.

'I can brew you a tea to help you sleep,' Leverett says.

I nod and mumble, 'Thank you.'

'Then I will focus on research,' Kate says. 'I will come over if I find anything, or you can come over any time if you think of something.' She pulls a book out from behind her and hands it to me. 'That reminds me, I grabbed this for you on the way out.'

It's a guide to lucid dreaming techniques.

I leaf through it. 'I may be a little ahead of this.'

'Of course, but there might be something in there you haven't read before. It couldn't hurt to have a look at the contents.'

I nod, but I doubt I'll find anything. It seems to be a basic introduction.

'Thank you,' I say again, a little clearer this time. I make a point to clear my throat so they think I just had something stuck before.

'If I find anything in my books, I'll let you know immediately,' Leverett says. 'Would you like me to bring the tea here?'

Deep breaths, Esta.

'I'll come over, if that's okay.'

I'll probably make a complete idiot of myself, but I have research to focus on. Hopefully that will help. Besides, if I don't get over myself and normalise being around him, I'll never be able to walk into his shop again, and that would be a terrible loss. I'm likely nervous because I've only realised my feelings for him yesterday. It'll get easier in time. Since he's so much older than I am—or at least I assume so, since I never asked his age—he's highly unlikely to be interested in me anyway, so I may as well accept my losses now and move on.

He smiles at me again, and all logic dies on the curve of his lips. 'I'll have your tea ready.'

Leverett excuses himself first. Kate follows right after. The moment Bonnie shuts the door behind them, she walks back to me and sits.

'So… that was weird.'

I look at her. 'What was?'

'You stuttering at Leverett.'

I can't keep a stupid grin off my face, so I press my lips together and look away. The latter makes it worse. Honestly, what am I, fourteen?

Bonnie's eyes widen. 'Wooooow.'

'Shut up.' I throw a cushion at her, and she giggles.

'I knew you were into older men, but—'

'Oh god, stop.'

I pray to any gods who'll hear me that Leverett and his superior vampire hearing are out of earshot. If he doesn't already know from my heartbeat, I really don't want to have to explain this conversation.

Bonnie scoots closer. I sag against her shoulder.

'You okay?' she asks.

I start to nod but then shake my head, which turns into another nod. 'I think so. We'll find something, right?'

'Yeah,' Bonnie says. 'Definitely.'

With all of us throwing ourselves into research, it has to be impossible to not find something.

'I don't want to think about it anymore,' I say. 'At least not for ten minutes. Tell me about your meeting with that diving instructor lady.'

Bonnie blushes. I'm not the only one who falls hard and fast. At least she has a chance with her lady. The realisation makes me happy and excited for her and sad for myself. I need to stop falling for the wrong people. But I don't want to dwell on it and ruin her excitement, so I focus on how the next time I fall asleep, I'll be armed with knowledge.

I try reading the book Kate gave me on my bed, but my small, inconspicuous dreamcatcher stares at me. Strings and sticks aside, it looks nothing like the creature that threatened me. I'm suspicious of it anyway, but I refuse to move. It's not the little ornament's fault. I won't be scared out of my own bed, damnit.

Maybe if Leverett were here with you...

Ugh. Sometimes I hate that little voice in my head.

Although the idea does sound nice.

He could hold you. He could whisper in your ear to chase the shadows away. He could kiss you, warm you from the inside out.

Alone in my bedroom, I blush the deepest shade of crimson at the idea of us both naked in this bed. Would he feel cold? Would he warm up if I stroked my hands over him?

I shake my head and leaf through the book to remind myself why I'm doing this. I hope Mischief is okay. She's not a real cat, though. She could have taken any shape, so maybe she can recover from something like this, too. Then again, who knows what that creature is capable of? I never thought anyone could just enter my dreams and mess things up, either, but here I am.

Bonnie sticks her head into my room. 'I'm taking Lady for a walk. Do you want to come?'

Stars, I'd love to go just to clear my head.

'More than you know,' I say, 'but I need to read this.'

Bonnie frowns. 'I'm sorry I can't do more to help.'

I shrug. The best people for this job are Leverett and Kate—I'm not sure even I will find much, and it's for my benefit.

'You do plenty,' I say. 'But maybe I'll sleep in your bed tonight.'

She laughs, and I feel lighter already.

'You can take me to that bookshop,' she says. 'I believe I was promised a vampire?'

I'm all too aware that my face is still red. 'I'll tell you next time I go.'

Bonnie nods. 'I'll come pick you up or something.' She hides her mouth behind her palm and giggles into it. 'In case you're too *busy* with each other to remember.'

I throw a pillow at her. 'I thought you were going for a walk?'

Lady barks from downstairs like she, too, was promised more.

'Esta and Leverett, sitting in a tree—'

I throw another pillow at her. 'Oh my *gawd*, go.'

She disappears with another giggle. Soon the patter of Lady's paws follows her out the door. Time to get stuck in this book.

From a glance over the table of contents, it does sound very basic, with chapters like "How Often Do We Dream?," "REM Sleep Explained," and "An Introduction to Freud's Interpretation of Dreams," but I feel like there is something worth exploring in here. I flick to the final chapter before the epilogue, simply titled "What Are Lucid Dreams?"

It begins just as basic. There's a quick introduction to what the term means, a brief history... but then I get hung up on a term I haven't come across before—dream walking. At first I think it defines lucid dreaming, since you could argue that it's just the dreamer consciously walking into their dreams, but then it mentions other people. Most of the two small paragraphs are speaking hypothetically, and some is almost dismissive, but the hairs on my arms are slowly rising.

Is that what the Dreamcatcher did? I have wondered if he came from outside my dreams, but a small part of me hoped that he was nothing more than a representation of my fear brought forth by Kate's and Leverett's warnings. It makes sense that he is an intense representation of my fear, but this paragraph...

If he really entered my dream from somewhere else, where is he? He didn't look human to me, but maybe he altered his appearance to scare me. He had so much control over my dreamscape, and even Mischief. Do I know him? Have we met and I somehow pissed him off? But the only people I've told about my photography idea are Kate, Leverett, and Bonnie, and I don't see them going to this much effort just to warn me. Leverett and Kate already told me in no uncertain terms how they feel about the project, and Bonnie is excited to see the end result.

This paragraph is painfully small, but now that I have a term, I can try to find a book about it. Maybe Leverett has already set one aside. Bonnie wants to meet me there anyway, and since she's already out with Lady, the timing works well.

I quickly text her to let her know where I'm going, and then I'm on my way with mixed feelings. I want to be alone with Leverett, but I don't want to be alone with Leverett. I want Bonnie to join five minutes after I walk in the door, and I want her to take her time. If I'm this awkward now, how will I behave once I'm in the shop? It'll be a disaster, but I have got to get over myself or I may as well never enter my new favourite book shop again.

My earlier worry plays on my mind for the first ten minutes of my walk. Did Leverett notice my heartbeat spike when he touched my knuckles? What if it wasn't an accident? What if he *wanted* to touch my hand, wanted to see how I'd react? I doubt that's right, though. Any vampire would have seen a lot in their time—little me is hardly interesting enough for someone who's been around this long. Not only that, but Leverett has known about all those other people for... well, probably since he was born, since he's part of that community. What can a young human like myself possibly offer?

I'm annoyed with myself for obsessing over this, and I'm annoyed with myself for assuming he's part of 'that' community. Vampires are their own people, just like humans are. It's possible that he hasn't always known after all. Then again, he wasn't surprised when I brought it up, and from what he told me about the war, it was pretty much the humans against everyone else.

I sigh and try to focus on my project. I want to people-watch as I walk, but the first few eyes I meet make me wonder if they're the Dreamcatcher, and I have to stop. None of them look like the rags/twigs/string figure, but what does that mean? He could have disguised himself so I wouldn't recognise him. There's a chance he isn't a *he* at all, in which case anyone I see could be the creature. When I look at it like that, it seems impossible that he's a real person outside my dreams, which means it really is just a fear. Hopefully Leverett will have a book or two that'll shed light on this mystery.

If the Dreamcatcher is born from a fear Leverett and Kate created, then facing the project is the only right thing to do. The more I develop it, the more I address what worries me. When I was a student, I had stress-nightmares before deadlines all the time. They weren't anything like the Dreamcatcher, but then this project is bigger. Is that part of the problem? If I've been putting too much pressure on myself with this project needing to be The One, then it makes perfect sense that my unconscious would reflect that. And if that's what's going on, there's really no reason at all to be scared of the big bad monster.

Something inside me twists at the idea—painfully, and jerky, like the Dreamcatcher's jarring movements.

Ironically, all this thinking relaxes me, right up until I reach Leverett's door. I take a moment as I remember where I am.

Alright, Esta. Calm the hell down. He's just a man—well, a vampire. He's just a vampire. You barely even know him. Don't get so worked up over someone you don't even really know and who you've noted yourself is unlikely to be interested.

One of these days, my pep talks will get better and actually start working. My heart races when I enter the shop, so today is not that day.

Leverett is reading a book behind the counter. He looks up when I enter and smiles at me.

Gods, he's handsome.

'I didn't expect you so soon,' he says. 'How are you feeling?'

I give him my best perfectly normal smile and shrug. 'Less scared and more confused.'

'It can't have been easy, watching him do what he did to Mischief.'

I shake my head. I really don't want to dwell on it.

'Can I offer you a tea?' Leverett asks. 'I have your leaves ready. Let me get them.'

I nod and wait by a bookshelf. There are a lot of occult books on this one. Are any of them relevant? So often when I studied, I would find single chapters or even just paragraphs in books that otherwise didn't look important to my research at all. Any of these books could potentially have the information I want, but I have neither the time nor the patience to read them all for that alone. I'd happily read them in their own right, but just to skim for something specific? No one has that kind of time, and I'm not the fastest reader, either.

Leverett returns and hands me two things—a bag of tea leaves and a book about astral projection.

'I don't know if it'll help,' he says, 'but I thought it might.'

I smile in thanks. 'It's worth a try. How much?'

'Nothing for the tea and nothing for the book. I said I'd help, and that's what I intend to do.'

My mind conjures up all kinds of ways to repay him, and I blush.

'Thanks, that's, erm...'

Now if my imagination could stop trying to picture him naked, that would be great.

'Are you alright?' he asks. 'You seem flustered.'

I blush deeper. 'Oh, yes, I'm fine!' I nod to the shop window. 'I walked—quickly, I mean. I hurried here. Just a little out of breath from that.'

He nods, but my gut tells me that he doesn't believe it. However, my gut also tells me to stand closer to him and accidentally brush my hand against his again, so maybe my gut is full of shit.

'Could I sit in the back to read it?' I ask. 'Bonnie asked if she could, erm, see you. She doesn't *not* believe that you're a vampire, she just has an easier time believing when she can see it. Seeing is believing, as they say.'

Oh gods, I couldn't have mangled that more. Something about him makes me want to use big words and sound important. I'm pretty sure I spectacularly failed on both counts. So, age and experience aside, here's another reason why he'd never be interested.

'Of course.' He waves me into the storage room. 'Would you prefer to sit upstairs? I can call you when your sister arrives.'

I nod to a chair. 'I can sit on the shop floor. Is it okay if I use that?'

His smile nearly undoes me. 'Of course. It'll be nice to have company for a change. We can discuss what we've learned.'

I remind myself that he doesn't mean *that* kind of company.

Leverett grabs the chair and sets it behind the counter for me. I thank him and sit.

'I haven't learned much since this morning,' I say. 'There was something in the book Kate gave me, though—something about dream walking?'

It's easier to focus on not making an idiot of myself when we're discussing something other than him. Odd, that.

Leverett sits next to me. So close our knees nearly touch. I press mine together, because if mine touches his for any length of time, I'll lose my focus again.

'I believe the book I gave you mentions something along those lines, too. Have you attempted astral travel before?'

I shake my head. 'I've heard of it, but lucid dreaming is something I've always just done. I never had to look into it.'

The two aren't the same thing, but I can see how they might appear in the same book. In a lucid dream, I become conscious in the dream. Astral travel is more like an out-of-body experience. My consciousness leaves my body.

'I wonder if that might be what happened,' Leverett says.

I begin to nod but bite my lip. 'I don't know. Whoever it was knew about my photography idea.'

'How many people have you told?'

'Only Bonnie, Kate, and you.'

Technically, I also told my boss that I want to create The Project over the summer, but I didn't have a starting point when I left work. She doesn't know my inspiration or the general idea.

'Before you ask,' Leverett says, 'vampires don't dream like

humans do, since we don't need sleep like you do, and if we did, we wouldn't use the time to enter your minds. We don't need dreams for that.'

I raise an eyebrow. 'But you *can* enter my mind?'

I've been calmer since we started comparing notes, but I go still now. Oh, fuck no. Please, gods, don't let him have read my mind. Not after he touched my hand. This is awkward enough as it is.

'Not in the way you think,' he says. 'I can't read your mind,' he says, right after I worried that he read my mind, 'but I can control you. I wouldn't, but many vampires do.'

'Why? What can we possibly do that you can't?'

Could a vampire have controlled a human general in the war to stop the fighting? I wasn't there, so I don't get an opinion. Still, I don't see many uses beyond that.

'It's rarely about ability,' he says. 'In the old days, before we went into hiding, some vampires controlled humans to make drinking easier. Others controlled humans for oral sex.'

I choke on my tea. Didn't expect that. I did not need the mental image of me on my knees before him.

'Sorry,' I cough out. 'Didn't see that coming.'

He chuckles, and I get hot. 'My apologies. It's still not quite a taboo subject, but it's more controlled than it was. Or rather, most vampires today don't see the appeal in humans.' My heart sinks. 'I mean no offense, of course.'

'None taken.' My heavy heart says otherwise. I guess that's the end of that, though. Maybe I can stop making an idiot of myself now.

'Those vampires who still prefer the hunt are closely

watched,' Leverett says, 'but I'm afraid many vampires, even the more agreeable ones, see humans as little more than food.'

I almost nod as if I get it.

'And you?' I ask. 'How do you see us?'

It sounds more desperate than I intended. Hopefully he won't read anything into it—after all, we've been talking a lot. I could just be asking as his friend.

'Like any other people,' he says. 'You're next to harmless to us unless many of you get together to hunt one vampire, but there's very little risk of that today.'

The bell over the door jingles, and I inwardly breathe a sigh of relief. I'm glad he sees us as people, but I'm even more glad that I can back out of this conversation now.

Bonnie waves and giggles at me. 'I hope I'm not interrupting anything?'

I blush deeper again. I will strangle her.

'Not at all,' Leverett says. 'We were just discussing differences between humans and vampires, and I gave Esta a book for research.'

He turns to me and smiles. I return it and pat the book like Bonnie needs proof that we haven't done anything filthy behind the counter. I'm pretty sure my obvious awkwardness is proof enough.

'I left Lady outside,' Bonnie says. 'I hope that's okay?'

Leverett nods. 'I prefer it.'

'Is it true, then, that dogs and cats don't like vampires?' I ask.

'Not at all,' he says. 'This collection is merely very old, and your Lady seems like the excitable sort. But no—dogs and cats have always been aware of us and learned a long time ago that we share this world. They react much the same to us as they do to you.'

I tick it off my mental checklist as Bonnie walks over and stands next to me.

'So, erm.' Her eyes flit from me to him and back to me. 'You said you're a vampire?'

He nods. 'I trust you won't send an angry mob after me?'

'What?' Her eyes widen. 'No! Of course not.'

Leverett turns into fog and reappears right behind me. So close I can feel his body heat, or maybe I'm imagining that bit. 'Then I trust Esta's judgement.'

My heart beats so fast I'm afraid it'll rip out of me. There's no way he doesn't hear it, but at least this time I can blame it on having been unprepared for his showing off. It would be a lie, but I'll stick to it if he asks.

Bonnie swallows so hard I see her throat move from the corner of my eyes.

'Okay. Yeah, me too.' Bonnie looks at me and smiles nervously. 'Esta has good judgement.'

Leverett flies back to his seat. 'I trust this is proof enough'—a lazy smile spreads on his lips—'or do I need to bite Esta?'

Oh *gods*. My poor heart will never beat normally again. Bonnie doesn't know that he doesn't drink blood, so her eyes go wider still. Then she giggles.

'I mean, if Esta wouldn't mind? Just so that I can be completely sure?'

Oh, she is *so* getting punched when we're home.

Leverett chuckles, and my vision goes fuzzy. I'm worried I won't be able to walk out of here. My legs don't feel up to it.

'He actually doesn't drink blood,' I say.

It feels like the lamest excuse ever coming from my slightly stuttering voice. I pray to every star in the universe that he doesn't hear it. If he does, I pray that he puts it down to fear—that's a normal response when confronted with the choice to be bitten by a vampire, right?

I try to hide behind a smirk. 'Good to know you're happy to sacrifice my neck, though.'

She giggles. 'You can never have too much evidence.'

I clear my throat. 'We should go.' I nod towards Lady. 'She's probably ready to go home now.'

'I'll keep looking,' Leverett says. 'If I find any more books, I'll put them aside for you.'

I smile at him and hope that, at least, doesn't look too awkward. I am grateful for his help. I just also need to learn how to be around him without letting my feelings get in the way.

If only it were that easy. If only we could choose who we fall in love with. I might have known better then. But he smiles at me again, our eyes meet, and I think that I'm dumb enough to have chosen him anyway.

When I awake in my dream, I'm at the shore of the void lake. Something feels off. I look around for Mischief, but she isn't here. My heart plummets. Does that mean the Dreamcatcher really did kill her? I try clear my throat, but no sound comes out.

My heart begins to race from the first onsets of panic, but I force my breathing to steady. I knew going to sleep would be harder tonight, so I'm not entirely unprepared for this reaction. Mischief isn't here because I'm afraid the Dreamcatcher killed her, that's all. I'm at the lake because that's where all this began, which makes the lake representative of every fear I associate with this situation. Dreams feed on fear if we let them. It's how they become nightmares. I've used my dreams to face my fears and heal myself in doing so for years, and I refuse to let some monster intimidate me now. My dreams belong to me and only me; I will not let anyone or anything take my control away.

I take a moment to ground myself. Mischief will come when I call her. She always has. There's no reason why she won't today as long as I don't give in to the nightmare.

'Mischief.' No sound leaves my lips, but I hope the intention is enough. I haven't had many opportunities to test the theory since she's always been there automatically, but… There's no sign of her. I know with dream certainty that she's alive, so why can't she come to me? Unless…

Maybe I need to find her. Maybe that's the point of this nightmare. Perhaps finding her would prove to my unconscious that I'm still in control by reclaiming my guide.

I nod to myself. I can do that. I have no idea where to start, but I can do it.

I close my eyes and say, 'Take me to Mischief.' Again, no sound comes out. My heart speeds up, so I take another moment to calm down. I will not panic.

If the point of this dream is me finding her, then I don't

expect my unconscious to simply take me to her because I asked nicely, but I hoped for a tug or a feeling to direct me. There's nothing. For the first time since I woke up in a dream, I don't just feel alone—I feel abandoned.

Why would Mischief want to be here with me when I can't keep her safe?

There's nothing much around me except for the caves behind me, and they're empty. Hollow. Try as I might, I see no sign of Mischief anywhere.

It hits me how alone I am. What if I never wake up again? I try to create a dream image of Bonnie, Lady, everyone I know including my parents, but none of them appear. It's just me and the vast, open space I can't fill.

My heart sinks. I feel as empty inside as I know the caves to be. Maybe that's all I am—a hollow shell inside someone else's dream.

There's a ripple on the lake's surface. I know Mischief can't drown and I know it's not her, but part of me is convinced that my dream guide is suffocating inside the obsidian void. I try to run closer, but the shore moves farther away. My steps are too small to catch up, and every step is heavier than the last, like I'm wading through a swamp.

Mischief cries out from inside the lake. 'Esta! Help me!' Her voice is muffled but amplified inside my head. While I still don't see her, I *know* her cries are coming from inside the lake, and if I don't hurry up, I'll lose her for real this time.

I try to answer, tell her I'm doing the best I can, but my voice is still gone. I try to scream just so she can hear *something*, but it makes no difference.

And then her cries for help turn into frantic meows, and it just about kills me. Silent sobs and screams escape me. Hot tears run down my cheeks. The harder I struggle, the deeper I'm digging myself. The more panicked my movements become, the smaller my chances of reaching her in time.

And all I hear are her panicked meows.

I scream again and throw all my willpower forwards. Something snaps; I fall towards the shore. I start to dig in the water like I'm trying to empty the whole damn lake one palm-full at a time. It isn't enough; there's something better I could do, but I can't think straight while Mischief is crying for me.

A hand shoots out of the water and grabs my wrist. A real scream finally tears out of my throat as I fall back and the fairy who had his wings ripped off drags himself onto the muddy shore. I'm sinking into it, but he doesn't have that problem. The ground firms for him and swallows me faster. I try to crawl away but instead back up into something. Arms close around my shoulders and my neck. Their skin is too white. They're dripping blood where big chunks are missing.

I curl up and will myself away. By some miracle it works, and I slip out of the dead man's grasp. It was pointless, though. All around me, the battlefield comes alive with dead werewolves, dead fae, dead vampires, and they're all closing in on me. There was no need to escape the dead man or the crawling fairy. There's nowhere I can run or fly where they won't get me.

Something grabs my ankle and pulls me onto my back. I must hit my head pretty bad, because I can no longer move it. I scream, but whose help am I expecting out here? No one's coming.

The fairy drags me to the lake. Water splashes my feet. Last time I dove in, it was silky and smooth like velvet. This time, it's real water, freezing and merciless, and he's pulling me into it. I try to struggle out of his grip, but my whole body has gone limp. My screams are swallowed by their moans and wails. They blame me; deep inside, I know they're right. I had nothing to do with their first war, but it won't matter when my art creates a second one.

Water closes around my face, and my scream drowns. The liquid is metallic, hot, thick. The blood of all the creatures who will die because of me. It burns my throat and sears my skin.

The grip on my ankle loosens. Far above me, I see light, tinged red through the near-black blood. I'll never reach it, no matter how hard I kick.

Wake up, Esta, I tell myself. *Just wake up.*

But I don't. I sink deeper every time I try to compel myself until finally, something shifts.

The Dreamcatcher appears in the distance. He's too far away for me to make out individual strings or twigs, but I see his disjointed movements even from here. Slowly, he comes for me. When he reaches me, he will destroy me.

'Is this sufficient warning?' he asks.

My voice is gone again, so I don't know how he expects me to answer. I can't even nod. All I can do is cry silent tears into the ocean of their blood.

'I know everything you do,' he says. 'I know you're still thinking about exposing us. Don't.'

Mischief's limp body floats into my vision.

'Curiosity killed your cat.' In one thought, he's right in front of me, so close I can smell and feel his foul breath on my face. 'Don't be its next victim.'

His rags wrap around my limbs. Sticks slide in under the fabric to keep my arms, legs, and fingers straight. I even feel them on my toes.

The Dreamcatcher vanishes. When he speaks, his voice fills the whole dead ocean.

'You will remember my warning. You will remember that I held back tonight. If you don't, I will do worse.'

He lets me float. For another felt century or so, all I can do is burn in the blood I spilled and drown in it.

CHAPTER
THIRTEEN

I wake up sobbing again. Since I was floating for a while, my screams have choked and fallen silent. Now, I'm numb. My pillow is soaked with cooled and still-hot tears. I didn't scream, so Bonnie hasn't come to check on me. Even if she had, I doubt the Dreamcatcher would have let her wake me. He was determined to keep me trapped. Bonnie could have shaken and slapped me, and it wouldn't have made a difference.

My heart is broken. Mischief deserved the world, and instead I brought her death.

Hers will be but the first if you don't stop, a voice that sounds too much like the Dreamcatcher whispers in my head.

My door opens a sliver and Bonnie peeks into my room. She sees my tear-stained face, lies down next to me, and pulls me into her arms. It's so comforting and full of love that I begin to sob again. Bonnie doesn't say anything, just lets me cry. I'm grateful for it. I don't want to have to repeat any part of that nightmare.

I'm not sure how long we stay like this.

'Would you like a tea?' Bonnie asks after a while. 'I think

the weather's cooled down some more. We can sit outside with it.'

I nod. She knows that a breeze always clears my head, though I'm not convinced it'll fix this no matter how much caffeine she adds.

Bonnie goes downstairs to prepare the tea, and I wash my face. I'm still shaken and fear I always will be, but the splash of cold water feels good all the same. I feel a little better when I join Bonnie in the kitchen, but not much.

Lady weaves her way through my legs until she looks up at me from between my knees and whines. She's so clever. Always knows when something is wrong. My heart breaks even more when I look into her eyes. The Dreamcatcher said he held back, that he'll do worse next time. He's already taken one familiar from me. Would he come after Lady? I lower myself next to her and hug her close, bury my face in her fur and inhale. Her doggy scent is one of the most comforting things in the world, and I soak it up as much as I can. If the Dreamcatcher comes after my dog, gods help me, *I* will become *his* nightmare.

'I've prepared a mug for Lady,' Bonnie says, 'but you know she won't drink it unless you pour it.'

I kiss Lady's head and let myself really feel her nuzzle. Mischief sometimes nuzzled me, too, but I never made a point of feeling it. Not like this. No pet of mine will ever go unappreciated in that way ever again. I will smother Lady with my love whether she likes it or not.

I stand and give Bonnie a tired smile. The circles under my eyes must be huge. Normally, I wouldn't care because a good night's sleep would fix it, but I'm not sure if I'll ever have one of those again. I haven't started my project, only considered options, and now I never will. The Dreamcatcher punished me anyway, for the mere thought. But how can I not think about it? I've only just learned about the Veiled, and I've done so little research. What does he want me to do? Wipe my memory?

'That bad?' Bonnie asks.

I nod as I pour water into Lady's cup. Lady trots after me and looks up at the counter with her heart's every hope in her big eyes. Nothing will hurt this dog. I will protect her with my life.

'Do you want to talk about it?'

I shake my head. Maybe talking about it would be the mature thing to do, and maybe I would realise the real meaning behind the dream if I did. Maybe it's nowhere near as bad as I think. But if I have to relive what I saw last night, I'll burst into sobs again, and I don't have the energy for that.

'Do you want to sit outside?'

I nod. Bonnie opens the door, and I follow her into the garden. She's right, it has cooled down. It even looks like it might rain later. Autumn is still a few months off, but I can appreciate the cooler temperatures and the refreshing breeze. I'm glad to see the end of this heatwave, except I don't suppose I'll sleep any better now it's cooled down. I whisper a request into the wind that it take the bad memories away.

Bonnie and I sit on the wall splitting our garden in two. Lady sits between us. Her tea hasn't cooled enough for her to lap it up yet, so I hold on to her mug for now. It's not much, but it's oddly reassuring that I can still hold on to something so small.

I sip my tea. 'How can I fight something that has taken complete control over the one thing I was good at?' My eyes glaze over as I stare at the grass. 'If even my dreams aren't safe...'

It's not supposed to be like this. Dreams are a representation of the unconscious. It's not right that someone else entered mine and did all those awful things. I feel violated. I pull my legs up and hug them close.

'I wish there was something I can do,' Bonnie says. 'I hate that I can't help.'

She scoots closer, and I lean against her.

'He threatened me again,' I say. New tears well up in my eyes, but I blink them away. I hate feeling like this. 'He keeps telling me to leave it alone, but I don't know what to do. It's not like I'm about to exhibit my photography project. I haven't even started it. I didn't ask to see the world for what it really is.'

Bonnie leans her head against mine. 'Would you have walked away from that lake if you'd known what would happen?'

I'm about to say that yes, of course I wouldn't have jumped in, but I hesitate. Not knowing about the Veiled was like living with a, well, veil clouding my vision my whole life. They've always been here, living alongside us in perfect peace. It's a whole part of being alive that I didn't see until I jumped into the lake. Would I really choose to not know all that? Would I really choose ignorance?

Lady whines up at me and huffs at the tea in my hand.

'Shoot, sorry.' I set it down for her, and she eagerly drinks the whole thing. Might Mischief have liked tea? It never occurred to me to conjure up a cuppa for her. It was always Lady's thing.

Would I have chosen knowledge, or would I have chosen Mischief? It's not a fair choice. There has to be a way to have both.

Only it's too late for Mischief, so I don't suppose I'll ever know. Will my unconscious create a new dream guide now? I don't want a replacement.

I shake my head. 'I don't know. I get the Dreamcatcher's point. There was a war, and they don't want another. Neither do I. If I'd immediately thrown myself into the project and shown the world the truth, it would have resulted in chaos. I don't want that, either.'

Bonnie smiles. 'I still can't believe that I've met a vampire, and I'm probably more open-minded than most.'

I return the smile, albeit a tired version of her own. 'But you do accept it. There are a lot of people who would start a fight over much less.'

She nods, and for a moment we just enjoy our teas. I close my eyes when the breeze picks up. Somehow it always knows when I need a little more comfort.

'I don't know what to do.'

The wind cools my fresh tears, and I let it carry them away. I'm so tired of crying and feeling sorry for myself, but every time I look at Lady, I remember Mischief, and then my eyes burn again. The lingering heat reminds me of the way the ocean of blood burned my skin and scalded my throat. Would I really cause that by taking a few pictures? Surely not. My mind has got to be exaggerating my fears. Isn't that all nightmares are?

The breeze is helping, though. What's been happening for the last two nights are either nightmares—horrifying nightmares, but still just regular nightmares—or someone really did enter my dreams, in which case they're likely acting out of fear. Surely a real person could be reasoned with? If I could meet whoever is behind this, if I could explain myself, show him that I mean no harm...

But I don't even know where to start with that. It's not someone I know, since the only people I've told wouldn't do this to me and are helping me fight this creature, so that means it could be anyone. That's a lot of potential people. How do I narrow it down from there?

'Was the book Kate gave you any good?' Bonnie asks. 'You were reading it yesterday.'

'It has potential, but I'll need to find the answer elsewhere. I'm hoping the book Leverett gave me will have that.' My foolish heart skips when I say his name.

'You're looking for something specific, then?'

I finish my tea. 'It said something about dream walking. I think the Dreamcatcher may not be a nightmare but rather someone who enters my dream from the outside.'

Bonnie's eyes go wide. 'Is that possible?'

I shrug. 'It's either that or it's really just a normal nightmare.'

She thinks for a moment. 'So... if he entered your dream from somewhere else, could I enter it, too?'

I'm about to dismiss it, but then I sit straighter. *Could Bonnie enter my dream?*

'I guess? I mean, if that's what he's doing… But I don't think it'd be easy, and you never remember your dreams.'

'Would I need to be asleep for it?'

'I've no idea.'

My heart beats faster at the idea. I don't want to bring her into my dreamscape when it's this fucked up, but what if we could fight the Dreamcatcher together, like some kind of superhero duo? The Dreamer and the Mermaid. Despite everything, I feel hopeful. Maybe I could bring Kate and Leverett, too—or actually, I don't want Leverett anywhere near my dreams. Fuck knows what my unconscious might show him.

Even if it's just me and Bonnie, two against one has to be better than one against one. She knows karate. It almost sounds unfair, except the Dreamcatcher isn't playing fair, either.

I look at Bonnie and feel a thin smile coming on. 'You might be on to something.'

CHAPTER
FOURTEEN

I call a crisis meeting with Kate and Leverett. He suggests having it in the back of his shop, and we all agree. Kate is already in town and promises to meet us there. The walk feels good, too, and by the time Bonnie and I arrive, I'm determined more than scared. Bonnie thought of a possible solution, and that's without her knowing a great deal about magic or dreams. That either means her plan has no chance of working or that she's a genius—which I've always known, of course. She's my sister; she's brilliant.

Leverett turns the Open sign around to Closed, and we head to the back. I half expect him to invite us upstairs, but he doesn't. Makes a girl feel special.

Kate sits on a box while the rest of us stand. My face burns whenever I feel Leverett's eyes on me… which is a lot, since we're here for my sake. I wish I could stand closer to him, but according to the Dreamcatcher I've already overstepped one big boundary, and I've lost Mischief as a result. I don't want to overstep another and lose what I have with Leverett next.

I tell them everything I told Bonnie. Then I suck it up and

decide to tell them a little more.

'There were corpses everywhere. I think they were all fairies, werewolves, vampires—you name it. They were reaching for me...' I ball my hands into tight fists when they start to shake. 'I heard Mischief crying for me.' New tears enter my eyes, and Bonnie shuffles a little closer. 'A dead fairy dragged me into the lake, but it wasn't like before. It was made of blood. I knew that it was theirs. All those corpses around me had died and bled because of me, and I was drowning in it.'

'Did the Dreamcatcher say anything?' Leverett asks.

'Just the same as before,' I say. 'He wants me to stop doing the project, but I'm already not doing anything.'

'Were those his exact words?' Kate asks.

I rummage through the memory. I'd hoped it had grown hazy by now as dreams do, but it's still perfectly clear.

'No. He said... Oh, what was it? He knows everything I do. He believes I'm still thinking about exposing them, but I swear I'm not!' Just knowing they are there is good enough for me. It's all I ever wanted. What's one photography project compared to this knowledge? I'd trade just about anything to keep it.

'It's not me or Kate you need to convince,' Leverett says. 'He sees your photography idea as a threat. It doesn't matter that you haven't started or that you've set it aside. The possibility alone scares him.'

My eyes plead with Leverett. 'Do *you* think I would do something like that?'

Leverett thinks for a moment. His hesitation hurts. 'I know you would never want war, but something like your project could have a ripple effect. It could easily grow out of your control, and then war might result from it regardless of your intentions.'

'He speaks out of fear,' Kate says. 'The Dreamcatcher, I mean,' she adds with a glance at Leverett. 'That's interesting, don't you think?'

I shrug. 'Does it make a difference? I don't know how to fight him, but'—I glance at my sister—'I told Bonnie about the dream walking I read about in the book you gave me. We're wondering if she could enter my dream like the Dreamcatcher did.'

Kate looks at her. 'I didn't realise you're an avid lucid dreamer, too.'

Bonnie shakes her head. 'I'm not. I don't remember my dreams that often.'

'It's a good idea,' Kate says, 'but given your inexperience, it would take a lot of practice. I'm assuming that Esta wants to sleep in peace again sooner rather than later?'

'But what else can we do?' I ask. 'I don't know what he wants from me. He can't expect me to just forget what I know.'

Leverett and Kate exchange a glance I don't like.

'There's a potion I could prepare,' Kate says. 'It would make you forget.'

A chill runs down my spine. Drink a potion and *poof*—memories gone. Just like that.

'Do you remember when I told you that vampires can control humans?' Leverett asks. 'I could command you to forget.'

'No,' I say. 'No! Absolutely not. There has to be another way.'

'I'm glad you don't choose ignorance,' Kate says. I guess that also answers Bonnie's earlier question, when we were sitting in the garden. 'I think Bonnie is on to something, but it will take time to prepare. How long depends on her natural ability.'

I nod, but my heart falls again. How many more nightmares will it take before Bonnie is ready? It's a plan, but how long can I last before I have a mental breakdown?

Bonnie looks a little disappointed, but asks, 'Where do I start?'

'You can begin by keeping a dream journal,' Kate says. 'The more you do it, the more you'll remember.'

Bonnie frowns. 'But I don't remember anything right now. What should I put? That I woke up and didn't dream anything?'

Kate nods. 'Yes, but rephrase it a little. If you repeatedly write that you don't dream, you'll train your unconscious to accept that it doesn't dream, which isn't true. Instead, write down that you don't remember anything. If you remember no more than a feeling or perhaps a colour, write those details down. It'll become more as you make it a habit.'

'Alright.' Bonnie looks at me. 'I'm sorry I can't do more right now.'

'No, it's fine,' I say. 'You're doing a lot, I mean.'

I smile. That everyone here has my back is encouraging. I already feel more prepared, even if all I can do right now is wait.

'Just think how cool it'll be when we can dream together.'

Bonnie grins. 'That's a neat goal to aim for.'

'I don't want to raise your hopes too high,' Kate says. 'Don't underestimate how long it'll take just to get to a point where Bonnie can try to enter your dreams. The actual act of visiting each other will also take practice. This might take months.'

Bonnie's smile falters, but I smile wider. It's a start. I don't know what I'll do tonight, but it's something to work towards. We now have a more defined goal than simply *defeat Dreamcatcher*.

'I will continue my research, too,' Leverett says. 'If I find anything else that can help you, I will make sure you get it.'

'Thank you, everyone.'

The words don't do how I feel justice. I'm beyond relieved that I don't have to tackle this monster alone.

'We have taken up enough of your time,' Kate says to Leverett. 'I'm sure you need to return to your shop.' She stands before he can object. 'We all have research to do, don't we?'

I want to stay longer—all day, if possible—but she's right. Bonnie will no doubt have questions about her new dream journal, too. I don't know how much I can answer since I've never had to make the effort, but I've read a few things now. If nothing else, I can help her get started, and who knows? My sister might be a natural after all. It's not like she's ever tried.

I turn to Leverett. 'I'll stop by when I can. Maybe tomorrow, if I'm not too tired to walk.'

It was meant as a joke, but I feel the grim reality settle over me as the words leave my lips. What if I can never sleep in peace again? What happens to people when they don't get enough sleep? I imagine being a little cranky would be the least of my problems, but looking into it isn't likely to make me sleep any better. I think I remember something about too much lack of sleep eventually killing a person, and that's after they lose their mind. I don't know how true it is, but is that what would happen to me? Is that what the Dreamcatcher wants?

I try not to dwell on it as we say goodbye to Kate and Bonnie and I go to buy her a notebook. I know the pen is supposedly mightier than the sword and all that, but buying a bit of bound paper doesn't seem like enough weaponry.

I'm scared to fall asleep again, but I don't have much choice. I'm so tired I could fall asleep standing up.

Bonnie offers to stay in my bed so she can wake me if I need it, but it would only make me more afraid to sleep alone until I can beat the Dreamcatcher. I also don't want to be in her way now she's trying to remember her own dreams. Getting woken up by a screaming me wouldn't help.

Of course, if I'm screaming the house down, she'll wake up anyway.

Still, if all I do is toss and turn, I'd rather Bonnie stays asleep and remembers a dream or two in the morning. Granted, waking up a few hours after falling asleep might just help her remember a dream then, but if she's busy comforting me, she wouldn't get to write it down, and then what's the point?

So, I decline her offer and instead hug a pillow like it's a lifesaver. I never thought my dreams would make me feel like

I'm drowning. With every passing night, I can't shake the feeling that I'm sinking a little deeper. My only hope tonight is that I haven't thought about doing this project all day.

As I drift off clutching the pillow, my mind wanders to Leverett and Kate. I'm grateful to have their help and I appreciate everything they're doing, but I also wonder if there are any Veiled with a natural talent for dreaming. Maybe the person living three doors down from me is some kind of dream fairy and knows everything there is to know, and I'm completely oblivious because we've never even met. Even if we had, I wouldn't have known they're a dream fairy. I let out a long sigh and feel myself falling. I visualise my dreams as they used to be—bright, purple-leafed, and controlled entirely by me. I hope it'll help me wake up in that version rather than in the Dreamcatcher's.

I fall. Most people panic when they feel this and jolt awake, but I've long accepted that it's just part of falling asleep—in fact, it's where that term comes from. Tonight, I wish I'd jolted awake.

I fall through a darkness that doesn't end. Something bad is waiting for me at the end of this eternity. The longer I fall, the surer I get. I don't want to land. I try harder to visualise the destination as my happy place, but I know deep down it won't do me any good.

'Surrender,' the Dreamcatcher whispers. 'You have no power while I'm here.'

'Yes, I do!' I want to say, but my voice is gone again. Still, I know he hears everything I'm thinking, so I add extra energy to my response in a pitiful attempt to assert my crumbling authority. 'These are my dreams! You don't belong here!'

'I belong in every unconscious. You can't fight me, Esta Anderson. Surrender, and I will leave.'

I doubt that.

'Very well.'

I wasn't aware of his presence before, just heard his voice, but his sudden absence rips a hole into the darkness. I fall into freezing water. Something grabs my ankle and pulls me under. This isn't my void lake turned to blood. The liquid doesn't scald me or burn my throat. Instead, it freezes my insides, and no amount of kicking brings me closer to the surface. Stupid me opens my mouth to scream, and ice rushes in—not cold water, but actual chunks of ice. They melt inside my throat. I can't swallow fast enough to return any semblance of warmth to it.

More hands grab my feet, my calves, and pull me deeper. Above me, red light reflects on the surface. Even the moon is bleeding because of me, I'm no longer desperate to leave the lake. I don't want to see what's above. Peace fills me, and my limbs grow still. My mind goes numb. Maybe this isn't so bad. The hands let go, and I sink ever deeper on my own. I don't try to stop it. I can't. I don't want to.

An invisible force grabs me and rips me out of the water. The sudden temperature difference makes me gasp. The invisible attacker flings me away from the shore, and I land with a bone-crunching *thud* on wet soil. It's tinted red, like someone soaked the land in blood. I push myself onto my legs to sit and finally stand, but everything spins when I do. My ankle hangs off my leg at an unnatural angle—the bone must have broken when I landed. I don't feel anything looking at it, but when I try to drag myself forwards pain erupts from my foot all the way into my spine like a fire raging in my veins.

I sit again. At best, I might be able to drag myself forwards with my hands, but I won't be walking anywhere.

I see a shape on the ground in the distance. It's too small to make out features, but the hair is dyed pink. Bonnie dyed hers the same shade years ago. She isn't moving.

Every instinct yells at me to help her, that I can save her if only I hurry, while a small pang in my heart admits that there's nothing I can do. Still, I will myself into the air. Still, I will myself to fly to her. Neither works. I can only do what the Dreamcatcher allows.

I start clawing my way towards my sister. I make it one metre before my hands feel raw—no doubt the Dreamcatcher demands they ache faster. Every inch hurts. I don't know if my hands are more covered in the soil's blood or my own, but I will not abandon Bonnie.

I'm determined to prove to the Dreamcatcher that he won't defeat me, that I won't back down no matter what he throws at me, but I remember Mischief's cries and am glad that she's not here. I don't care what I saw—I don't believe for one more second that he killed her. She's an idea, a dream guide born from my unconscious. She's only gone when I don't need or want her anymore, and that'll never happen. Mischief isn't dead. The Dreamcatcher is keeping her from me.

Something clicks in the back of my mind, but nothing changes and I can't put my finger on what it is. I feel like I've made progress, even if I don't know the details. It's not enough for me to be comfortable with what's happening, but there's hope. I can defeat this.

But even as I think it, the Dreamcatcher knows. The ground disappears, and I fall again. It happens so fast that I can't even blink or comprehend what's going on. I land on something sharp, and pain sears through my chest, straight through my heart. The pain is so intense that I can't even scream. My arms don't work, my hands don't respond. Above me, I see myself reflected in a gigantic mirror that fills the void I just fell out of. My blood drips off the stalagmite I'm impaled on and falls onto my face. Some runs into my mouth. It's bitter and rotten.

I hear a growl behind me. In the mirror, I watch the dead from the battlefield pull themselves out of the ground and towards me. I scream again, but no sound leaves my mouth or even my chest. The stalagmite destroyed my heart as well as my voice. I can only watch in silent horror as the dead begin to pull the flesh off my bones. I feel the *pop* when one rips my leg out of its socket.

Just when I think I'll never be sane again, the dead around me disappear. Darkness swallows the ground, and the stalagmite vanishes, too. I fall onto my back and stand. My wounds are gone. My body is whole again. I run my hands all over myself, but I don't even have a scratch. The change is so jarring that I burst into nervous, sobbing hiccups.

Then something tackles me, and I'm on the ground again. My face hits the bloody soil first. Whatever is on me is heavy, and it's not making any efforts to get up. But it's also not clawing at me or otherwise attacking me, so I count my blessings and turn around even though I know better. This is

176

the Dreamcatcher's doing after all. Whatever it is won't be a relief.

I spot a bit of fur and freeze. I no longer want to see. I don't want to know. I want to wake up.

Now.

But the Dreamcatcher controls my body and makes me turn around.

My dead dog lies on top of me.

I start to shake, and another silent sob-scream tears out of me. *This isn't real, this isn't real, this isn't*—

The Dreamcatcher isn't done, though. Another weight falls onto us. Bonnie with her beautiful pink hair, matted red-brown from a head wound. More weight falls on us and I feel my ribs crack. Kate, her throat cut. Leverett, decapitated. His head lands next to mine. I turn my face away so I don't have to see. But the other side of this nightmare isn't much better, because the Dreamcatcher is watching from my other side.

'What do you want from me?' I try to scream at him. My voice still isn't working.

I scream even more when he doesn't respond. There's nothing more he can say to me. I know his terms, I just don't understand them.

He disappears, and the weight of my dead friends and family disappears with him. I sink into water. This time, I don't try to kick or make it back to the surface. It's dark down here, and I don't want to see any more.

So I let the depths swallow me and numb my pain.

I don't get up when I wake. I even pretend to be asleep when

Bonnie checks in, but under the duvet, my eyes are wide open. I don't risk falling asleep again.

I hate feeling like this—useless, powerless—but I don't know how to fix it. It'll only get worse the more nightmares the Dreamcatcher forces on me. Even if I tried to stay awake, my body would force me to sleep sooner or later. No amount of tea can make this okay again.

My dreams have always been my one safe space from everything else. That they are worse now than anything real life can throw at me is a violation unlike anything I could have imagined. It feels wrong on a primal level that someone else has forced their way into my unconscious and shown me all these horrors. It's wrong that I'm afraid to fall asleep.

The Dreamcatcher keeps asking me to stop. I'd comply if I knew what he wants from me. If he simply doesn't want me to do the project, fine. I meant what I told Leverett and Kate, and I can't take another night like this—and it's only been three nights. What he's doing to me goes beyond a bad night's sleep. I'd give anything to make it stop.

Anything but my memory.

It's the one thing that makes me who I am. Everything leading up to this moment right now has shaped me. My memories are proof of everything I've experienced, everything that got me *here*. Knowing about the Veiled is part of that. If I lose that... Would I still be Esta Anderson? Leverett and Kate offered me their ways out, but I don't want those. Hell, Leverett is proof that humans and vampires, at least, can live side by side just fine. Why can't the Dreamcatcher see that?

It doesn't matter, though. The problem is that he doesn't

see what I see. He claims to be in my head and know everything I think, but he doesn't know that I don't mean them any harm. Or maybe I'd cause it anyway and he knows that, too. That doesn't matter, either. He won't stop until I give him what he wants.

Fine, I think and hope he hears it. *I said I won't do the project. I won't bother you or anyone else in your community. Happy?*

There's a dull ache in my gut, and I know it's not enough for him. Nothing short of forgetting everything I've seen will be enough. But even if I took up Kate or Leverett on their offer, would it do? I haven't stumbled upon one fairy or one vampire by accident. I unlocked something in my mind—something that has always been there—and I don't think forgetting a few days of my life would change that. Which means I'm back to the beginning. If only he spoke clearly... but I suspect that he thinks he does. After all, he asked me to stop. What could be clearer than that?

Unless... I curl into the duvet. He doesn't expect *me* to stop, does he? Does he need me to stop existing? Do I need to die before he's happy? Bonnie knows what I've seen, but without the same ability, she doesn't see the world as I do. She saw Leverett because he can bring out his fangs and claws at will, but other people, like fairies, use magic Bonnie can't see through unless they take their magical barrier down. Kate doesn't see them unless they choose to show their true selves. Leverett is part of that community himself. None of them would be a threat to the Dreamcatcher.

Maybe that's what he wants—for me to stop seeking them out. I've been wanting to meet more, so perhaps that's the issue. My gut constricts further. *Please, don't ask me to stay away from Leverett.* Even if we never go past friendship, I can't bear the thought of never seeing him again. My feelings aside, he's been a great friend, and his bookshop is a treasure trove. Surely me buying books from him and having a chat doesn't endanger the delicate balance the Veiled have created for themselves? The bookshop isn't exactly some hidden secret. Anyone can walk in and buy any book they want.

New tears soak my duvet. I don't have the energy left to sob, so they fall in silence. Not even my shoulders move as I cry into my sheets.

All this knowledge. All this truth all around me. If I give it all up… It would break me. I would hate not knowing again how much more there is to everything. It's not about being special—the only human with this kind of insight—and entirely about finally seeing the world for what it really is. I have the feeling that I've barely scratched the surface. If Kate or Leverett helped me forget, or maybe both of them for good measure, I'd never know what I'm missing. Would I always have a strange kind of homesickness for what I've lost? Maybe the part of me that called me to the lake has always known, and that's why I've craved something more all my life. Would they wipe out even that? I jumped into the lake, and my world filled with colours I never knew existed. If I let them take it away, my world would be different shades of grey again. I can't bear that thought.

Images of my dead family and friends flash into my mind, and I pull the duvet away so I can focus on something, anything, that's not the memory of my broken dog.

Nothing short of choosing ignorance will satisfy the Dreamcatcher. He has lived in my dreams so far, but if we're right and he's entering from the outside, then he's a real person. He could make my nightmares real if I don't listen to him.

I shake my head to get the grim memories out of my head. No matter what, I'll lose. It's not worth anyone's lives.

Maybe the grey veil won't be so bad as long as I have Bonnie and Lady.

CHAPTER

FIFTEEN

I drag myself out of bed and jump into the shower. The moment the water hits my face and runs over my body, I feel lighter. I ask the water to wash away my fear, and I take longer than usual to make sure all the negativity is really gone.

The longer I let the water cleanse me, the clearer my mind becomes. I think back to the tree and how I saw the magic flow through it. Can I really give that up? I don't want anything to happen to anyone because of me, much less my family and friends, but it seems I have no choice. It's either ignorance or death.

I hold my face under the stream and beg it for answers. Kate taught me years ago that knowledge is power. The Dreamcatcher knows what I think; therefore, he has power over me. I know about the Veiled; therefore, I have the power to start a war. But there are so many spaces in between. There must be something I'm missing that would let me fix this without sacrificing anything.

I don't want to fall asleep again. My best option is to find a solution before that happens, and it needs to be strong enough that the Dreamcatcher will accept it. The only problem is that I'm exhausted. Last night was the third without good sleep, and I'm feeling it this morning. I haven't stopped yawning since I stepped into the shower. My whole body is sluggish. If I'm to power-research today, I'll need a lot of tea.

To start with, I need to find a way to take back control over my dreams. It's my unconscious; the Dreamcatcher has no right to it. I *will* take back control tonight, and then I'll kick him back to wherever the hell he came from. Surely there's something I can do in my dreamscape that he can't? I don't accept that Mischief is dead, either. She's there somewhere, I'm sure of it. I just need to find her. Since I don't have a clue how I'd start researching this, I guess I'll figure it out when I'm dreaming tonight. The thought scares me, but it also gives me power. Maybe it's okay to not always have all the answers before I act—it's fine to learn by doing and improve as I go. The Dreamcatcher just poses a bigger challenge than I'm used to, but I'll conquer this, too.

Once I've done that, I'll need to somehow make a deal with the Dreamcatcher so he leaves me the fuck alone. Leverett and I are proof that our two people can get along. Other Veiled live amongst humans every day and go about their business. Many, if not all, likely have human friends, and they get along just fine. Their wings or their magic shouldn't change that. If it does, the friendship was never real to begin with. You either accept each other or you don't—it should be that simple. I can't be the only human who wants peace.

The Dreamcatcher has shown me horrors unlike any I've ever imagined, but he hasn't really *done* anything yet. Bonnie and Lady are fine and healthy. Kate isn't dead, and Leverett's head is still attached to his neck. Would the Dreamcatcher come after us outside my dreams? If he's that worried about the consequences of my knowledge, why not just kill me? I don't think he's a murderer or he'd have come to me outright; instead, he gives me nightmares. He doesn't want death, either, at least I hope he doesn't. I've thought before that he's acting out of fear, and that he hasn't hurt me outside my dreams further makes me think that he's just defending himself. The nightmares he gives me seem extreme, but if he believes that he's fighting to save the lives of every Veiled... Is there really such a thing as too extreme? He's not just trying to save ten or a hundred lives. He's trying to prevent slaughter, maybe even genocide. If I were in his place, can I honestly say that I would stop at some gruesome mental images? Since he knows my thoughts, he must know where I live—the thought alone scares me—but he hasn't knocked on my door.

Unless he has and I didn't recognise him. For all I know, he's the guy who delivered our pizza the other night.

But there's no point dwelling on that, because it doesn't change the overarching truth that he hasn't hurt me or anyone I know. He's threatened me clearly enough, but I don't believe he would resort to physical violence. We both want the same thing—peace and a good night's sleep. Although...

Clearly, the Veiled want to stay hidden, so it makes sense that he hasn't attacked me in the open. It would be a lot harder to hide if he conjured shadow monsters in Eastgate's high street. If Bonnie found me dead, there would be an investigation. Openly using magic like that would invite more conflict, probably riots as humans struggled to accept the truth forced on them so violently. Eventually, if it escalated enough, it might lead to a war declaration. So, all things considered, of course the Dreamcatcher has only come after me in my dreamscape. Given my habit to become conscious in my dreams, I was probably an easy target.

I don't know if I can ever forgive him for the nightmares he's put me through, but if he is desperate and does it because he genuinely believes that I'd get a lot of people killed... He would never have put me off with a mildly troubling dream. It had to be as wild and as awful as he could make it or I wouldn't have listened. As it is, I'm listening and I'm still looking for loopholes.

My fingers have pruned from my long shower, so I finally turn it off and inhale the steam for extra courage. I've no idea what I'll do, but it'll end tonight. If I don't pass out from exhaustion sooner, I have roughly sixteen hours to make it happen.

I'm so determined that I call Kate and Leverett while I still have a towel wrapped around me. Bonnie peeks into my room while I get dressed and raises her eyebrows.

'Slept well?'

I pull my shirt over my head. 'No. It was awful, actually, but I have an idea.' I grin and realise how tired my eyes are. 'I've just called Leverett and Kate over. How did you sleep? Dream anything nice?'

I don't want to rely on my sister's progress, especially because it's only been one night, but having her there for additional backup wouldn't hurt. We've always been a good

185

team. I know we'd kick dream-butt, too.

But she shakes her head, and I deflate a little.

'I think I dreamed of something brown? I woke up really craving coffee, though, so I might just have been thirsty.'

I shrug. 'It's a start.' Frankly, I'm surprised she remembers that much already. 'I appreciate that you're doing this.'

I join her in the door, and she pouts.

'I hate that I can't look out for you in your dream.'

I smile. 'One day.'

We're family, after all—not by blood, but by choice. Our sisterhood is all the stronger for it. We protect each other. Soon, even dreams won't stand between us.

Unless they destroy my sanity first. I frown at myself; I won't let it get that far.

Since Kate lives next door, she's over within minutes. Since Leverett can turn into fog and fly, he arrives within minutes, too. Maybe once this stress is over, I'll ask him how it works, but it's not my priority right now, curious as I am.

We assemble in the lounge—Bonnie and I sit next to each other, Kate sits on the spare sofa by the window, and Leverett leans against the wall next to the fireplace.

'Thank you for coming so fast,' I say. 'I have an idea, but I want to hear if you found anything more first.'

'I gave my most useful book to you,' Kate says. 'Have you two made progress?'

Bonnie shakes her head. 'I'm trying, but all I remember from last night is a colour, and I think I only remember that now because I wrote it down and told Esta about it.'

Kate gives her that patient teacher smile I adore so much.

'No progress happens overnight, as they say. Keep trying, and you'll improve. If you expect to master a technique that many don't even believe in after one try, you will find only disappointment.'

My sister nods, but I know the look on her face well enough to know that she's still upset. Kate is right, though—she'll manage it, but it'll take time. Time I don't have.

'How did you sleep last night?' Leverett asks.

The memory of the dream shoots back into my head—the bloody fur, the severed limbs, the *pop* as my own limbs were torn off. I close my eyes and shake my head like that'll make it go away, but the darkness only makes the memory more vivid.

'Not well,' I say. 'If I don't figure out a way to pacify the Dreamcatcher tonight, I...' What more can he show me? My nightmares have got worse every night for the last three. What's the next step up? I can't even imagine it, but I bet he can.

'Is that your plan?' Kate asks. 'To pacify him?'

I nod. 'There must be a way. He and I want the same thing.'

Leverett crosses his arms. 'Are you sure it'll be enough? I agree that peace is the best way forwards, but from what you've told us, I'm not convinced he'll see it your way.'

For a moment, I agree. Leverett has experience and knowledge to put us all to shame. He has seen more, done more. But as far as I know, he's never fought a monster in his dreams. He said himself that he's never heard of this Dreamcatcher, so in this, at least, we're all on the same page.

'What do you think I should do if he won't listen?' I ask.

Leverett's heavy look speaks for itself. 'If you can't reason with him, kill him. It's either that or your sanity, or am I wrong?'

I shake my head. 'No, I think you're right, but I don't like it.'

Would killing the Dreamcatcher be like killing another person? I have no proof that he exists outside my dreamscape, only guesses. When I've faced other fears, I conquered some of them by killing them or jumping right into them, but I can't shake the feeling that the Dreamcatcher is more than an idea. If that's true, if he's a real person… and no problem is solved by killing someone. His death would just be the first in the very war I want to avoid. I don't think the Veiled are watching or even aware of me, but if they are or find out in the future, I don't want me killing one of them to be my introduction.

'Whether you like it may be irrelevant,' Kate says. 'There are many beings in this world that are so single-minded in their purpose that they can't consider other options. Think, for example, of a starving wolf in the wilds who needs to feed her pups. Will she try to tear you apart to survive another day, or do you think you could reason with her?'

'That's not the same thing,' I say. 'The wolf needs to act on instinct, but I already talked to the Dreamcatcher. We had a brief conversation. And what would happen if I shared my food with the wolf and brought more? Wouldn't she see that I'm a friend?'

My mind is reeling. I'm close to an answer, I can feel it—I just wish I knew how to take that last step.

'The Dreamcatcher is trying to protect himself and the entire Veiled community, isn't he?' I say. 'Much like the wolf wants to protect her pups. I just need to show the Dreamcatcher that I'm not a threat.'

'I believe you already tried that and he didn't listen,' Kate says. 'What makes you think tonight will be any different?'

I almost shrug, but it won't help my case. Then I shrug anyway, because pretending a confidence I don't have won't help, either.

'I don't know,' I say. 'Perseverance? Maybe, once he sees that I'm not changing my mind despite the nightmares—'

'And how many more are you willing to endure in the meantime?' Leverett asks. 'Beings like the Dreamcatcher are much older than you can imagine. He might have seen the war. In theory, he could even have fought in it.'

A chill runs down my arms. That would explain his persistence. I've only seen fragments, but the brutality in them is enough to turn my stomach and break my heart. If the Dreamcatcher lived it, fought it, I can't blame him for trying so hard to prevent it now. What's one human's sanity compared to the lives of millions?

Leverett probably thought his point would put me off, but I'm more determined to fight for peace than ever. I can't be weak when I face him tonight. I need to show him that we can fight, too, and that we don't need violence to do it.

'I agree,' Kate says. 'It's good to see you wish for a peaceful solution, and I encourage it, but you need to be careful. As Leverett said, this being could be ancient. You might not be the first lucid dreamer he's encountered—in fact, it's unlikely. No matter what you want to tell him tonight, he's no doubt heard it all before.'

I know they want to help, but I feel discouraged nonetheless. What if he *has* been in this situation before? What makes me think I'll be different?

'We don't know how those times might have gone,' Bonnie says. 'So what if he's done this before? We don't know that. Isn't it also possible that those other people attacked him?'

I nod, grateful that my sister is the voice of reason. Calling her that feels unfair, though. All three are voices of reason. They have slightly different views and concerns, but they're all valid and we all want the same result: an end to the us-and-them thing.

I shiver and hug myself. When I put it like that, it feels much too big for me. Aren't there people better qualified for this kind of diplomatic mission?

'I wish I could do more,' Leverett says. He turns to Kate. 'Is there a way for me to enter her dreams?'

'No!' I blush. I may have protested a little too fast.

I'm not naive—chances are he already knows how I feel from my pulse and heartbeat alone—but if there's any chance he thinks that I'm just nervous because he's a vampire and I'm a weak little defenceless human, I'd much rather go with that illusion. If he sees my dreamscape, though, there's no way he'll keep believing it. I have too little control over my dreams right now to risk it. Any other time, I'd choose what to show him, and even then who knows what might surface anyway? Dreams are too closely tied to instinct and symbolism. Bonnie is welcome any time—she already knows everything about me.

I clear my throat and hope they believe my excuse. 'I mean, I need to do this on my own.'

I like what I have with Leverett. It may not be everything I want, but it's a good compromise. I'd much rather have his friendship than nothing at all. The Dreamcatcher has scarred me enough already—I won't let him ruin this, or I'll start taking it personally after all.

'Think about it, though,' Bonnie says. I tense. 'Wouldn't it prove your point to the Dreamcatcher if you and a vampire argued your case together?'

I blush harder, because she's got me there. How do I argue with that kind of sound reasoning?

Leverett nods. 'I think so, too. It may be all the proof he needs.'

I shake my head, hoping I'll think of something as I talk. 'He already seems to know everything I'm thinking. He knows we're friends, and he doesn't like it. I doubt both of us talking to him would make a difference.'

There, that'll do. Thank you, timely inspiration.

Leverett frowns. Is it my imagination or does he look disappointed? Did he *want* to see my dreamscape? What on earth for?

'I see your point,' he says. 'You shouldn't go in without protection, however.'

'It's not a bad idea,' Kate says. 'I would prefer the process to be natural, but perhaps I can help it along a little.' She nods to Bonnie. 'I can't promise it'll work right away, but there's a potion I can brew that would help you sleep and encourage more vivid dreams. I can also mix in something to improve your awareness. If you sleep close enough to Esta—which you already do—she might be able to pull your dreaming consciousness into her own.'

My heart begins to race. It seems too good to be true. 'Why didn't we do this right away?'

'Because we don't know enough about Bonnie's natural ability. There are no dangers as such, but it's always better to let things happen organically. Given the situation, however, I believe it's better to give you all the help we can.'

Bonnie looks between me and Kate. 'So there's no danger that I'll get stuck in Esta's head?'

I smirk. That's not a place anyone wants to get lost in.

'No,' Kate says. 'At most, you'll feel disoriented when you wake up. You might feel out of sorts the next day. I can teach you reality checks if you're unsure whether you're still in Esta's dream.'

I snort and smile at Bonnie. 'Don't worry, my dreams are way weirder than this room. You'll know the difference.'

Her uncertainty disappears when she smiles.

'I was going to teach you different reality checks anyway,' Kate says. 'I wanted to wait until you had more experience remembering your dreams, but I suppose it won't hurt to teach you now.'

I yawn. 'Sorry. I'm not bored, just tired.'

The lack of good sleep is really beginning to take its toll on me. My whole body feels heavy, even with caffeine. I hope I'll be able to sleep after all. It's not comfortable to be physically tired except for a caffeine-induced racing heart.

'I will need time to brew the tea,' Kate says. 'I can have it ready in a few hours, but the herbs and roots need time.'

I don't think I can stay awake that long. Kate said I'll be

able to pull Bonnie's dreaming mind into mine. Can the Dreamcatcher call awake-me back into my dreams in a similar way? I don't know enough about him to know what else he's capable of. He's already seized perfect control of my sleeping mind, so maybe he can control my waking mind to a degree, too. It's a scary thought. All the more reason to get this over with.

'I will stay here,' Leverett says. 'I've brought a few books so I can continue my research while you sleep.'

I blush again. It warms me that he wants to watch over me—and yes, I know that's technically not what's happening. The more I nod off, the harder it becomes to reason. I hope it'll be easier to make sense of… things… once I wake up in my dream. This won't go anywhere if it doesn't.

'Thank you.' I nod to him and to Kate so they know I mean both of them.

'I wish I could get back to sleep,' Bonnie says, 'but I'm too awake right now. I've had a strong coffee.'

I wave her off. 'Don't worry. If this works, you might never need to visit my dreams.'

She pouts. 'Oh. It sounds cool, though.'

I think I laugh, but my vision is getting heavier by the second.

'I'll go to bed. Good night.'

But even as I speak, I struggle to keep my eyes open. I'm faintly aware of someone touching my arm—Bonnie, I assume—and then I'm out.

CHAPTER
SIXTEEN

I'm an unsettling combination of tense and determined when I wake up in my dream. I'm scared to see what'll greet me this time, what it'll grow into, but I won't let it get to me. No matter what the Dreamcatcher throws at me, I'll be ready. I won't take his bait. I'm here to talk. The only fighting I'll do is fighting for peace; although, that in itself sounds like a contradiction.

But I arrive in nothing. There's no landscape, just a black, starless void. Something like fog curls around my ankles, but my gut tells me it's something else, something I don't have a name for.

Ahead of me stands the Dreamcatcher, completely still except for his twisting, snapping movements like dry branches in autumn. He stays where he is, and I'm grateful for it. He's perfectly unsettling from all the way over there, with his strings and sticks hanging off him and poking through his rags.

I take a deep breath in to steady myself. If he won't come any closer, I should. I'm here to prove that we can coexist without fear or conflict; if I stay over here, I'm not sending the right message. I also can't move closer too soon, though, or I might come across as aggressive. I want that even less. So I stay where I am, too. At least for now.

My heart hammers from the memories of the last three nightmares. My eyes dart around like I've missed the big bad monster about to throw itself at me, but everything is perfectly still except for the Dreamcatcher's jerky movements and the not-fog around my ankles. My breathing feels out of place here. Maybe it's a good thing that we both stand out like this. In a way, I feel like it connects us.

'Thank you for not throwing me into another nightmare,' I say. Hopefully my gratitude will help smooth things over. 'I appreciate it.'

'You want a chance to speak, though I don't know what you believe can come of it.' His face doesn't move when he speaks. His voice simply *is*, like it itself is the air in this space.

The hairs on my arms stand on end. 'If you know I want to talk, you must know what I'm hoping for.'

A jerk that looks like his neck snaps sends my heart racing faster. What *is* he? His neck snaps the other way, but there's no sound to make me flinch. It's silent, like all his other movements. His other limbs twitch, too, but it looks subdued, like he's trying to still himself. Like he's as tense as I am.

'You want peace,' the Dreamcatcher says, 'but we cannot risk it.'

I grit my teeth. What more can I do except tell him?

'You've seen who my friends are, how I've reacted to everyone else. I haven't taken one step towards war.'

'The vampire. The witch. They are but two people—hardly

representative of us all.' In the blink of an eye he stands right before me, so close that I can feel his foul breath on my face. 'There have always been those such as you, humans who want to live alongside us without endangering us. You're not the first.'

'The war.' I shiver. Neither of us want to relive that dream. 'I don't want a repeat.'

'None of us do, but that was merely the first and therefore the most important attempt. We saw that day that we and you cannot live together like you want. The hope of one human isn't enough. Your curiosity is dangerous. It scares us.'

I swallow. What can I say to that? His fear is justified, but is it justified of *me*?

'I'd never do anything to harm you.' But even as I say it, my argument feels weak.

'Then let me give you another example. You apply for employment. You're not the only one to be called forth, but you're the only one you know personally. You don't know who the other candidates are, but you want the job. Maybe you perform a spell for luck or success. When you get the job, you are grateful, but what of the single mother who misses out and will now continue to struggle? What of the man with depression who has been without employment and income for years and counted on this opportunity? Does your success not also continue their misfortune?'

I don't know what to say to that. It's not a fair comparison, but I see his point.

'This isn't like that,' I say. 'There is more than one position available here. We can all benefit.'

'Can we?' The accusation in his voice takes my breath away. Like the war has already begun.

'Tell me why we can't.' I have a feeling I'll regret it, but if I can't make him understand, I may never sleep peacefully again. 'Leverett showed me that he's a vampire because he trusted me, and I haven't betrayed him.'

'That you make the same point again shows me that you haven't understood my example. Your actions have consequences, and yours more so than others'. Your intentions may be commendable, but what about the people you entangle in your web? Can you honestly say that Bonnie will forever keep this secret? What happens when she meets someone and trusts them, only to have her trust betrayed?'

I'm about to object—Bonnie would never do that to me or to them—but how sure can I really be? It's not about her; it's about what love does to anyone. I confided in her because I trust her, but couldn't she do the same with someone else one day? She's interested in the diving instructor. Who hasn't done or said something stupid when they were newly in love? I know Bonnie wouldn't spill this secret on their first date, but what about the fifth? What about their tenth wedding anniversary? At what point do we deem our trust in a loved one strong enough to survive anything?

I don't know what will be in ten, twenty years from now. I do know that the Veiled are scared of what my next move will be and that I'll do anything to protect them. It's not their fault that I wandered into this. I won't make it worse for them than I already have just by asking questions.

But I refuse to forget, too. I can't endanger them if I don't know that they exist—

But I also can't help.

'Your silence is your answer,' the Dreamcatcher says.

I shake my head. 'I won't do the photography project. You have my word.'

I mean it, but my gut says it isn't enough.

'You saw what we endured,' he says. 'We cannot risk it. It is regrettable, but…' His twigs turn into sharp spikes, and his threads wrap around my limbs. 'You don't know the minds of humans. Your open-mindedness is an outlier. Even if it isn't and humanity truly is on the turn, we cannot risk it. Our children depend on us. Hiding is preferable to extinction.' He pauses, and I hold my breath. 'We regret the necessity, but killing one human is preferable to killing most of you and dying regardless. Perhaps one day, the time will be right, but we don't believe this time has come yet.'

His spikes shoot through the rags and into my skin. The Dreamcatcher holds out another, right before my head. I want to plead my case one more time, but rough fabric closes over my lips and over my eyes. I don't know if he thinks I'll be more relaxed if I can't see the weapon coming, but it has the opposite effect. I writhe in my prison. No matter how hard I try to thrash, his sharp twigs dig in deeper and his strings hold me tighter until I resemble one big, human dreamcatcher. I barely feel the pain from the spikes in my limbs. Is he numbing the pain to make it easier for me, or am I too high on adrenaline to feel it? Maybe he thinks he's being merciful, but it doesn't feel like he's taking pity on me.

My heart feels about ready to tear out of my chest as his

rags silence my protests. All I can do is wait for the end to come, but I'll be damned if I go down without at least trying… even if I can't move a muscle in the tangle he has woven me into.

Something heavy hits my chest.

I jolt awake to a shoe on my heart.

I gasp out a strangled sob when I spot Bonnie in the door with her arm still raised and shock in her eyes. My sister just saved my life by throwing a shoe at my boobs.

'Oh my god, Esta! What *was* that!'

'Wha—' I fly out of my bed and run over to her, desperate to be away from the Dreamcatcher. I know he is in my unconscious and therefore follows wherever I go, but in my head, in that moment, he lives under my bed *and* in the dreamcatcher hanging over it. Bonnie didn't throw the shoe for the hell of it, so maybe he really does live under my bed like every child's nightmare come to life.

Bonnie flings her arms around me and inspects my face. 'Are you okay? What happened? What was that?'

Her eyes are wide, and her hands are flailing like she doesn't know what to do with herself.

I pull her into my arms again, hoping it'll steady both of us. 'I think you saved my life. I went to bed to talk to the Dreamcatcher, it didn't go well, and then you threw a shoe at me. I should be asking *you* what happened. What was what?'

Without letting go, she whispers, 'Something was sitting on your chest.'

I pale. Every hair on my body stands to attention. So, she really did see him. In my room. *On me.* But where did he go?

Is he still watching us? I'm terrified as well as relieved. I do not want that thing in my house, let alone in my bedroom, but if he's here, I don't have to defeat him in my dreams. Kate is next door, and Leverett is still here. We can do this together.

I pull away a little so I can look into her eyes. I hope it'll make me more aware of my surroundings, just in case the Dreamcatcher is about to pounce on me from my wardrobe.

'A creature made of sticks and strings, yes?'

Bonnie shakes her head. 'No, a woman. I think.'

I pale further. What woman? I've thought of him as male, but maybe I was wrong. We can be anything we want to be in dreams. Maybe she altered her appearance and her voice to fool me better.

My heart plummets into my gut. Could it be Kate? She seems to know how to get into other people's dreams, and she excused herself to go next door when I fell asleep on the sofa. She discouraged me from the project, and she's one of the only few people I told about it.

The other pieces don't fit that theory, though. Bonnie knows what Kate looks like—she wouldn't have said *a woman*, she'd have said *Kate*.

'Who was it?' I ask.

Bonnie shakes her head again. 'I don't know. I've never seen her before. I only came to check on you because Lady was barking up the stairs.'

Despite my reasoning, I breathe a sigh of relief that she didn't name our lovely neighbour. I don't know what I would have done.

I also make a mental note to hug my dog and cook her food

myself for the next month.

'Well...' I look around my room again, but there's no sign that anyone else has ever been in here. 'She's gone now. Is Leverett still here?'

Bonnie nods. 'We were both researching stuff after he carried you to bed. I don't know what he's got, but I—'

She giggles when I blush. It's not as cheerful as her laugh usually is, but after the dream I just had and the revelation that something has been sitting on me while I slept, it's the best sound I've ever heard. It doesn't distract me from her words, though. Leverett carried me. In his arms. To my bed. And I missed it because I passed out. Bloody typical. Of course, if I hadn't passed out already, I probably would have when he picked me up, so this feels less embarrassing. But he was in my room, with me in his arms. I spot everything that's wrong with the space—the laundry basket with yesterday's underwear on top; the lacy bra slung over my bedpost for today; the socks in the corner; the cute panda pjs on the floor next to the bed.

'Did he really carry me to bed?' I whisper in case he's listening and laughing to himself downstairs.

Bonnie nods; her grin reaches her eyes. I just know I'll never get the red out of my cheeks.

'Well, this is awkward,' I say. 'I was about to suggest going downstairs and asking if this woman sounds familiar to him, but on reflection, I don't think I'll ever talk to him again.'

My sister's giggle sounds more like herself this time. 'If it helps, he came back downstairs too quickly to have gone through your underwear drawer.'

'Mhmm.'

I don't want to point out that he's a vampire and can bloody fly and turn to fog. For all I know, he was *inside* my underwear drawer.

I don't have much choice if I want to solve this, though. We go downstairs, Bonnie giggling again and glancing at me when she sees Leverett which I'm *sure* he doesn't notice, and I try my best to act normal.

The four of us sitting in my lounge drinking tea and discussing my nightmares is beginning to feel worryingly normal. Lady lies across my legs like she's trying to protect me, and I cling to her fur. It might be nice to talk about different things one day, even if it's just the weather. Right now, I need to know why there was a woman sitting on my chest and how I can win an argument with the monster who sees me as too much of a threat to consider killing me.

I tell the others everything the Dreamcatcher told me.

'Would it have… worked?' I ask, not quite ready to say *killed me* out loud.

It doesn't reassure me that Leverett and Kate look as lost as I feel. I figure I really would have died, because why else would the Dreamcatcher have done it? The thought is terrifying, though. Turns out, if you die in your dream, you do die in real life provided it's because the Dreamcatcher shoves his sharpened twig into your brain.

'It's hard to be certain,' Kate says. 'We know everything we know about the Dreamcatcher from you.'

'You said he mentioned others?' Leverett asks.

I nod. 'He said there were others before me who wanted peace, but it never worked out.'

I think back to how he trapped me, how I resembled a me-sized dreamcatcher. Is that what would have happened to me if Bonnie hadn't intervened? Would I have hung over someone's bed one day to keep their nightmares away? There are too many dreamcatchers in the world for them all to have someone's soul trapped in them, but what if some of them do? The dreamers would never know.

I hug myself and turn to Bonnie. 'Thank you for throwing the shoe at me.'

Kate looks at my sister. 'Can you describe the woman you saw on Esta?'

'I didn't get a good look at her,' Bonnie says. 'It was dark since the curtains were drawn, and I didn't take a moment to memorise her face. I just saw her and threw the shoe.'

'And because of that, Esta is alive,' Leverett says. It makes my heart beat a little faster that it matters to him. 'I'm sure you saw enough that we can piece it together.'

Bonnie takes a second to think. 'She was crouched over, I think. She looked a bit like those medieval pictures of hags, I guess?'

I'm not sure if this is helping, but as Bonnie said, she didn't take a moment to take in the woman's features.

Kate looks thoughtful though. 'I've never heard of a Dreamcatcher in relation to her, but I do know of the Mara.'

Leverett nods. 'That's my thinking, too.'

A shiver runs down my arms, because I've also heard of her. None of it is good.

'Doesn't she cause nightmares?' I ask.

'Yes, though it's unclear how,' Kate says. 'I wonder if she works by putting the Dreamcatcher into your dreams and controlling him from the outside.'

I pale. 'From atop my chest…' Has she been sitting on me every night? I shiver again.

'It seems likely,' Kate says. 'There are many writings on her, at least. We'll make sure you're better prepared next time you fall asleep. You may not be able to reason with the Dreamcatcher, but you might be able to talk to her through him.'

'Won't she already know of our plan?' I ask. 'She knew everything else before I told her—it's why she entered my dreams in the first place. If she's out here, why don't we just ask her while I'm awake?'

It would be so much easier if I had everyone's support with me and wasn't trapped in a nightmare for it. Now that the Dreamcatcher and I have talked it out and he's decided I'm too much of a risk anyway, I'm afraid he won't hold back, if he ever did. He was set on killing me last time. I'd rather not fall asleep and see if I wake up again.

But Kate shatters my hopes with one shake of her head. 'The Mara only exists on this plane when she enters your dreams. She needs the physical connection to get into your unconscious. The easiest way to describe it without going into too much detail is to say that she lives on another plane of existence. She only visits this plane when she enters someone's dreams.'

So there goes that idea.

'That doesn't mean you'll have to be helpless, though,' Kate says. 'I prepared the tea for Bonnie. If she's willing to try joining your dreams, the next time you sleep will be your best chance.'

Bonnie nods. 'Yes, definitely. I want to help.'

'What do we need to do?' I ask. I can't imagine she'll drink the tea and automatically hop into my dream. There must be something I need to do on my end, or maybe she needs to do something once she's dreaming. Given her inexperience, she might not become lucid enough to realise, so it'll likely fall on me... and I'll likely be busy with the Mara and the Dreamcatcher.

'You will need to pull Bonnie into your dream,' Kate says. 'I can't guarantee it'll work since neither of you have done this before, but it's worth a try.'

I'll just be glad to not be alone; although, as Kate said, there's no guarantee. I might waste my time trying to somehow find Bonnie's unconscious from inside my own and not see an attack coming because of it.

'We can watch over you from here,' Leverett says. 'If the Mara appears again, I won't let her near you.'

I smile and blush. If he's there from the moment I go to bed, I'll probably be too nervous to fall asleep. The thought of anyone standing next to my bed as I drift off is weird no matter who it is, but I guess it beats someone climbing onto my chest after I've fallen asleep.

'And I'll watch over Bonnie,' Kate says.

Bonnie looks at her. 'Over *me*?'

'If the Mara isn't listening right now, she'll still know what

Esta knows as soon as she enters her unconscious. She might come after you herself or send someone else to make sure you can't join Esta.'

I swallow. I hadn't considered how this might put Bonnie in danger.

'It's okay if you don't want to do it,' I say. 'We know it's a Mara now. With all of you looking for her out here, she might not be able to send the Dreamcatcher after me.'

Bonnie pouts. 'No, I want to help. I was promised dream adventures.'

Despite the situation, I grin. The Mara won't know what hit her if we both show up. Except she will, because she'll have access to my memories. But she won't know how good a team Bonnie and I are, and Bonnie knows karate. I can't picture the Dreamcatcher coming at me with punches and high kicks.

'If this goes well, we can make it a yearly thing,' I say. 'Like a yearly dream adventure for your birthday or something.'

She grins, too, and hope fills me again. We can do this.

'There's one thing you should consider,' Leverett says. 'We've been talking like the Dreamcatcher is only in your mind because of the Mara, but it's possible that he's a separate being. She might have put him there, but it's possible that he doesn't need her control to act. Even if we keep the Mara away from you, he might still throw you into a nightmare.'

I nod. I figured as much, but hearing it confirmed doesn't make me feel better. This whole time I thought I needed to fight one enemy, but turns out, there are two. Who have I really failed to convince? The Dreamcatcher or the Mara? If I win one over, might it convince the other? Maybe I've been doing this all wrong. Maybe I should be talking to the Mara instead. But she won't show up while I'm awake, and I don't fancy having a chat with her sitting on my chest. So, there's really no point dwelling on it.

'Do we all know what we're doing?' Kate asks.

'Yes,' I say, but I'm only half-sure. 'Bonnie and I fall asleep, and I pull her consciousness into mine.' So far, so seemingly impossible. But I have read about dream walking before, so if other people manage it with years of experience, I can totally pull this off on my first attempt. That seems reasonable. I gulp and hope necessity will speed things along. 'Kate and Leverett will watch out for the Mara, and Lady will be the goodest girl and keep an eye out, too.'

My dog barks, and I feel better already.

'Then only one question remains,' Leverett says.

'And what's that?' I ask.

'If they still won't listen to you and decide there's only one way forwards, are you prepared to kill them?'

I swallow. I guess I'll find out the hard way.

CHAPTER
SEVENTEEN

Bonnie and I end up sharing the tea Kate has prepared. She drinks most of it, but I take a few sips. The tea is meant to help her sleep and become conscious inside her dreams, and while I'm so tired that I won't need any help falling asleep, it can't hurt to have the extra push once I'm dreaming. Maybe it'll strengthen our connection, too.

Bonnie lies down first. She's worried she won't be able to sleep so soon after getting up this morning, but Kate's tea is strong—Bonnie is out within five minutes. With Kate and Leverett waiting in my room for me to fall asleep already, I'm the one who's struggling. My eyes are heavy and I yawn every two seconds, but it's impossible with both of them staring at me. So, eventually, I ask them to wait outside. If the Mara shows up, maybe she'll make a sound. Even if she doesn't, Leverett and his sharpened vampire senses are waiting for her. They'll know when she's here.

Lady was harder to convince, but since I'm used to her sleeping on my bed, I don't mind that she's staying. Leverett and Kate leave my room, Lady curls up next to me, and I'm barely aware of any of it as I drift off fast. I'm scared. The Dreamcatcher might attack me the moment I wake up in my dream, or he might be willing to talk again given my backup. With Lady's warmth next to me, it's hard not to feel at least a little comforted. My dog is watching over me. If the Mara shows up, it won't go unnoticed.

I'm still willing to talk, but Leverett's words haunt me as I begin to fall. Am I prepared to kill them? I'm not a murderer. I've never even held a weapon. They've given me terrible nightmares, but it's clear to me from my last chat with the Dreamcatcher that they don't want to hurt me any more than I want to hurt them. Everything they've done and shown me, they've done in self-defence. But what if the Mara arrives and immediately goes for my dog? If she hurts Lady, it'll change everything. I hope she'll stay away. I've no idea how this other-plane stuff works, but if she can see me from there, she must know how well guarded I am today. Even if she hurt my puppy, she'd have an angry vampire and a determined witch after her. The Mara doesn't strike me as stupid.

So I'm equal parts determined and scared as I fall into my dream.

I land on a pile of corpses, bloody and with their limbs, wings, fangs ripped off. It makes my eyes water and a sob shoot into my throat, but I blink the tears away and swallow my cry. The Dreamcatcher is fighting for his and everyone else's survival—I don't blame him for going in hard.

It's not easy to stand amongst all this death, but it either happened an extremely long time ago or it hasn't happened yet. In fact, if I look closer, the pile I landed on is made up of my friends, family, and other people I saw in the park. That won't work on me today. I know they're fine right now. One advantage to lucid dreaming is that I *know* it's a dream.

I don't want to give away that I'm alright, though, so I stay on the pile, try not to think about where I am, and try to reach Bonnie. I have no idea where to go from there. If Mischief were here, she'd know what to do and could guide me, but I don't know where she is, either.

Although...

How often have I reminded myself that Mischief is an idea? She's a dream guide—more spirit than physical cat. And if I'm sure that the Dreamcatcher didn't really kill her, that she still exists within my unconscious...

She must be in here somewhere, and that means I can reach her.

I close my eyes and turn my attention inwards. *Mischief.* In any other dream, she would hear me call and come, because that's how dreams work. Today, like the last few dreams, there's no sign of her, but I know she can hear me. As something that exists in my unconscious, she can't very well not hear me. We can choose to block out bad memories, but we can never truly forget anything—every detail of information gets stored away. Therefore, Mischief is around here somewhere, I just need to figure out where.

Or I would if my mind were a physical room. That's how I thought of it before, like the Dreamcatcher has taken my dream guide and locked her in a prison, but the only buildings here are the ones I create, and they are all ideas and memories, too. This is why dreams are like smoke—if you don't make a point of remembering them as soon as you wake up, if you try to force it, they'll only disappear faster. And then it hits me:

That's why I haven't been able to find her. I tried too hard, pictured the wrong thing. There is no prison. There is only me.

'Mischief!' I call her again, out loud this time to give voice to my intention. It's not usually necessary, but I figure the extra step can't hurt today.

The ground around me begins to rumble. By saying her name out loud, I've given myself away. The Dreamcatcher would always have caught on—I smirk to myself, partly because of the bad joke and partly because I'm starting to feel like I'm taking back control—so I might as well hurry things along.

I move down the pile and steady myself as the ground shakes harder. I had a *lot* of nightmares about erupting volcanoes as a child; I'm surprised he didn't use it against me sooner.

This time, though, I'm not scared. I refuse to let whatever misery he throws at me consume me.

'Mischief!'

A sob escapes me when soft fur strolls around my legs. I look down to see her reach up to me with one paw.

'Esta!'

I hold out my arms. She jumps into them. I've never wanted to bury my face in her fur so badly, but the hug will do for now.

'Do you know what to do?' I ask her.

Just in case the Dreamcatcher doesn't know yet, I won't voice my plan with Bonnie. I don't need to—Mischief knows all the hidden nooks in my dreamscape.

She nuzzles into my neck, and I cradle her sweet little head with one palm. I *knew* she was alright, but nothing beats the relief of seeing her alive and well.

'Yes,' she says.

'What do I do?'

The ground cracks under us. I move my right foot onto the same side as my left foot, just in case the Dreamcatcher rips the ground into opposite directions.

'She's your sister,' Mischief says. 'You know her energy. I can taste something else on the tea Kate made you— something powerful, but I'm not sure what. But Bonnie is trying to reach you, too. Can't you feel it?'

I want to ask what in the cosmos Mischief is talking about with the tea. I want to say that no, actually, I can't feel a bloody thing, but then…

Esta?

I hear her.

Mischief digs her claws into my arm. 'Grab it!'

I have no idea how, so I let my dream certainty take over. We never question how to fly when we dream or how to move from one impossible location to the next—we just do it. So, I don't focus on not having all the answers and hold on to Bonnie's call.

'I'm here,' I say, like I'm in my bedroom and she's in the bathroom. Like there isn't an impossible void between us.

But maybe it's not so impossible after all, because I open my arms, will Bonnie into them…

And there she is, stumbling into me like she tripped over

her own feet. We both jump away from each other, arms spread wide, and eyes wide in amazement. It worked. Kate is a genius.

I scream at Bonnie in surprise and amazement. She returns the sentiment. Neither of us can believe we're in my fracturing dreamscape together.

She finds her corpse a few feet away on the other side of the crack, and her eyes widen.

'Ignore it,' I say. 'Look at yourself as a reminder that you're alright. Even if there was a sword sticking out of you, it's only a dream.' A mischievous smile spreads on my lips. 'We can do anything here.'

She mirrors my smile. 'Even defeat the baddies?'

'Oh yes.'

All around us, corpses come to life. Bonnie pales, but I'm so over it.

Until they moan and start to run towards us.

I freeze. Figures that the Dreamcatcher would send running zombies after me.

Bonnie grabs my arm and backs away slightly. '*What do we do?*'

Damned if I know. Zombies aren't supposed to be able to run, but of course the Dreamcatcher isn't fighting entirely fair. I really need a moment to think, but of course, running-bloody-zombies don't give me that time. *Maybe* I can reason with the Dreamcatcher, but these things? How the hell am I meant to reason with the frenzied undead?

One throws itself at Bonnie, and her training kicks in. She rams her elbow into its head, and it bursts into blood and bones and something slimy I don't want to think about. Bonnie gasps. We both stand and stare, horrified.

Another zombie charges for her and grabs her wrist when she instinctively punches it in the face. The asshole gnashes at my sister.

Her eyes widen, and she pales. 'Esta—'

Fuck. I shouldn't have brought her here. What if the Dreamcatcher kills her? What'll happen to her if the next zombie actually takes a bite out of her? I'm used to this weird feels-real-but-isn't of my dreams, but it's all new for Bonnie. Even if whatever injuries she might get in here don't translate to her waking body, what if they mentally scar her? What if she'll be forever afraid to close her eyes?

I take a deep, stuttering breath. *Get it together, Esta.*

We can't kill them all or I'll prove that the Dreamcatcher is right to be afraid. If there really is another way, now's the time to find it.

'Don't kill them,' I say. 'I mean, I know they're dead already, but don't kill them again. Just knock them out.'

I can see her gulp, but we both ready ourselves. She flows into her karate stance, and I test how much control I've regained.

'This is your dream,' Mischief purrs at me. 'There's nothing you can't do.'

What I really need right now is to keep the zombies away without hurting them. The Dreamcatcher needs to see that I'm serious about peace.

I focus on freezing the zombies in place. It's not as easy as it should be, but about half, at least, stop moving. The rest move more slowly until they resemble the slow beasts zombies should be—those things have no business being fast. A few still reach us, but Bonnie knows just where to hit them so they stagger and crumble to the ground.

Once all the zombies are either frozen or knocked out, we stare at each other.

Bonnie breaks into a nervous giggle-fit. 'We are so cool!'

We high-five each other.

I laugh. 'Yes, we are!'

I dread to think what else the Dreamcatcher has for us. By now, he must know that I'm regaining control fast. How easily will he be able to tear it back now that I know?

'We just want to talk!' I shout into the air. I could have thought it and he'd have heard me, but I want to make sure that I get my point across. 'We don't want to fight!'

The ground opens up and reveals rivers of thick, flowing magma. Bonnie screams and grabs my arm, but I will a red meadow with yellow poppies and tiny sunflowers into being under our feet, just because I bloody can. It's not much, but it feels good to have this much control again.

It's tiring, though. If I don't end this quickly… I don't know how long we have.

'I know you work with the Mara,' I say. 'Could I please talk to both of you?'

I feel weirdly awkward phrasing a polite request in the middle of the rupturing ground and the sea of magma beneath us, but I don't think I'm in a position to make demands just yet.

The air shifts. I hear twigs snap before I see him. Bonnie

and I spin around.

The Dreamcatcher stands before us.

Bonnie gasps. I wonder what she smells since she loves liquorice.

'It's not that simple,' he says.

'Sure it is,' I say. 'Please. I promise I won't talk to any of the Veiled unless we become friends first, and then it'll be their decision to reveal themselves. I won't tell anyone. I won't do the project. Please, I can keep a secret.'

Especially when it ensures the safety of... shit, how many of them are there? There must be millions worldwide.

'It's true,' Bonnie says. 'I've never guessed my birthday or Christmas presents. She gives nothing away.'

I love that this is her proof.

'It's not my decision,' he says.

I nod. 'It's the Mara's, right? Bonnie saw her.'

He hesitates. I figure it's because he didn't think I'd know the truth, but then he says, 'No.'

Bonnie and I glance at each other.

'So... if it's not the Mara... All this was just you? How can it not be simple, then?'

'No,' he says again.

I frown. Bonnie pouts, annoyed that we were wrong.

'I don't understand,' I say. 'If this isn't your idea and it's not the Mara's, whose is it?'

'Maybe it isn't the Mara,' Bonnie says. 'We decided so quickly; we might have missed something.'

The air shifts again, and a woman appears next to the Dreamcatcher. She stands hunched over. Her eyes are clouded like she's blind. Bonnie was spot on—she looks exactly like a hag from medieval paintings.

'You guessed correctly.' She sounds like a caring grandmother, but there's an edge to her voice. As sweet as she may sound, I need to remember that she caused all this... or maybe she didn't, if it's neither of their idea.

'That's her,' Bonnie says. 'She was on your chest.'

The Mara points a bony finger at my sister. 'You claim to want peace, but your first reaction was to attack me.'

Bonnie blushes and averts her eyes. 'I didn't expect to see anyone on Esta's chest. I'm sorry I threw a shoe at you.'

'What will happen when you face a monster worse than I, girl? What will you choose then?'

'I don't think you're a monster,' I say. 'You're just trying to survive.'

Bonnie nods. 'That's why I threw the shoe—I was trying to protect my sister.'

'And yet the shoe could have dealt real damage,' the Mara says. 'Everything we do here won't leave a physical scar.'

I bite back a response. It might not leave a physical wound, but what about mental scarring? The Mara must know this. I don't believe for one moment that she isn't aware of the power she wields.

'Could it, though?' Bonnie asks. 'Kate says you're not... of this... plane...'

'That doesn't mean we can't be hurt, girl. Even if it were true, you didn't know it at the time.'

I'm worried that we've already messed this up. The Mara doesn't sound like we're negotiating, more like she's explaining why we're grounded and any further argument will only result in a longer sentence.

'We could have attacked the zombies,' I say. 'We didn't. Neither of us hurt them. That must count for something?'

Next to me, Bonnie nods vigorously.

'Indeed, it should,' the Mara says.

'But as I have explained,' the Dreamcatcher says, 'it's not our decision. We were asked to eliminate the threat to our safety.'

The Mara nods. 'To disobey would be unwise.'

'But who—' I bite my lip again. Demanding answers isn't the way forwards; instead, I decide on a different approach. 'Never mind. You don't need to tell me. You've made your point that your community wants to remain hidden, and we understand that. If your… employer… doesn't want to talk to me, I won't force it. I only ask that you don't—' *kill me* gets stuck in my throat. It feels odd to beg for my life in this way— casually, like we're discussing how heavy the rain will be tomorrow. 'I want to help you stay safe. We both do.'

I don't know what else I can do. If they still don't agree… Leverett's question echoes in my head. I don't want to kill them. I don't even want to hurt them. Every movie I've seen, every book I've read, seems to require that the hero kills their enemy. I don't feel like a hero; I'm one of their villains. Death shouldn't be necessary. It's not healthy to need or expect it, and since I'm not a hero by any means, I don't see why I should conform to that expectation. This isn't a story. I'm not a character in some book. I'm Esta Anderson, and I just want to accept the world as it is, not as it's been taught to me.

Mischief paws at my leg. I glance at her, our eyes meet, and I know what she's thinking. There's one way I haven't considered.

'If my word isn't enough, what about theirs?' I ask, cautiously optimistic. 'Leverett and Kate are in my house right now. Talk to them.'

This conversation concerns them, too. It shouldn't happen without them. Even if Kate herself isn't technically one of the Veiled, she's still more involved with them than I am.

'Your two friends are not representative of every Veiled,' the Dreamcatcher says again. 'I have explained this. Talking to them will not change anything.'

'Won't it?' the Mara asks. 'Should we not talk to other Veiled if given the chance?'

The Mara and the Dreamcatcher exchange a glance. The Dreamcatcher hesitates. For a moment, none of his sticks move. Then—

'Yes. But do you want to risk her wrath?'

For a moment, I think he means me, but then the Mara slowly shakes her head.

'I don't want to risk a war,' she says. 'I also don't want to stand in the way of fate.'

'You know what she demands. We mustn't upset Balance.'

I want to say that I don't want to upset the balance, either, but I feel that I shouldn't interrupt. They talk about balance like it's something they revere, and after all these years of peace, I can see why. I wouldn't want to ruin that, either—I *don't* want to ruin it.

'Are we puppets to move whenever her fingers pull the

threads?' the Mara asks. 'Can we not think for ourselves?'

The Dreamcatcher goes still except for his unsettling twisting and twitching. When he turns what I think is his gaze on me, I don't feel reassured.

'Very well,' the Dreamcatcher says. 'We will hear your friends on this matter.'

'But how—'

I wake up with a gasp. I hear the door fly open, and something heavy—I'm assuming the Mara—leaves my chest. I grip the sheets to ground myself. I'm back in my bedroom. Is Bonnie awake too? Is the Mara still here?

I turn my head to the side to find Leverett pinning the Mara to the wall. He has his back to me and blocks her face from me, but I hear his growl in his voice.

Lady is growling, too. From behind the bed and with her head between her paws.

'What did you do to Esta?' Leverett snarls.

Oh, be still my heart.

I jump out of bed and put my arm on his shoulder. 'It's okay. They, erm, suggested we all talk about this.'

He glances at me over his shoulder, and my heart melts further. He looks so relieved to see I'm alright.

Leverett drops the Mara and fully turns around to me.

'When I heard you gasp I thought… You're really alright? Is it over?'

My smile over his honest concern is genuine. This is why I don't want to lose him, even if he never returns my feelings.

'Not quite.' I look past him at the Mara. 'Are you hurt?'

She chuckles. The sound reminds me of my grandma. 'I'm

not so easily injured. It's unexpected to see one of the Veiled defend a human like you just did.'

Leverett straightens and apologises. 'The Veiled and humans help each other all the time.'

'Ah, but do they?' the Mara asks. 'Would that still be the case if the humans knew what the Veiled truly are?'

I am not having this discussion in my bedroom.

'You two go ahead downstairs. I check on Bonnie. We'll meet you there.'

But even as I leave the bedroom, Bonnie's door opens and she and Kate greet us. We're a rather weird procession down the stairs: Bonnie and myself in the back, then Kate, then the Mara, Leverett, and finally the Dreamcatcher, leading the way like he knows this house as well as I do. Given that he knows everything I've ever thought and seen, he probably does. It still feels strange to have him leading the way, but I'm not about to object; I'd rather not turn my back to him, and there's never been a worse time to be petty about walking order.

The Mara and the Dreamcatcher stand in the middle of the room with us forming a sort of half moon before them. She and Kate exchange a glance like they're equally curious about the other, but it doesn't last. I guess Kate was wrong about one thing: the Mara does have a physical form on this plane, at least for a little while.

'This human suggested we hear your thoughts on this matter,' the Dreamcatcher says. Here, in my living room, he looks disturbingly still. Like the wind that usually moves his strings and snaps his twigs only exists in the dreamscape. It's an unexpected kind of wrong. Somehow, his jerky movements were more natural.

'I'll admit to being intrigued,' the Mara says. 'Are you aware of how little you know, I wonder?'

'Anything you can share with us would be appreciated,' Leverett says.

And for a second, I think they'll tell us more, but then the Mara shakes her head.

'It is not for us to say,' the Dreamcatcher says. 'We risk enough by having this conversation.'

'Then I won't pry,' Leverett says. 'I know Esta. I've never felt anything but comfort around her.'

My heart can't take much more. One more sweet word from him and I'll die after all. I know he's only saying what they need to hear, but I know Mischief won't let it go for a good few months regardless.

'I am more than happy to teach her too,' Kate says and gifts me one of her smiles full of mystery. 'She's a fast learner, and she has a good heart. I will guide her.'

The Mara chuckles again. 'Yes. That is what you do, is it not, Mother—'

'I believe she deserves to keep her knowledge,' Kate interrupts. There's something else in her voice, but I'm not quite sure what. Like she's warning the Mara to not say another word. Like she's worried the Mara might continue. As it is, I don't understand why the Mara called her Mother, but this isn't the time to be nosy. Not when I'm trying to convince everyone that I can keep what I've learned without bugging the Veiled for more information.

'We trust your word,' the Dreamcatcher says. My heart

jumps again, until he turns his attention to me. 'You don't know the danger you are in, human.'

I scoff, hoping it sounds light-hearted and not like I'm making fun of them. 'There's danger every time we leave the house. We humans don't have eternity or hundreds of years. Any day could be our last.' I look at both of them so they see my sincerity. 'I want to embrace the world as it really is, and I want to see it for myself. All of it. Kate is a great teacher. If her guiding me'—whatever that means—'is a condition you can accept, then I accept, too.'

'And I believe it worth noting,' Leverett says, 'that humans were not the only aggressors in this war or in the years since. The humans attacked first, and I don't blame any of the Veiled for being scared. But let us not forget that the Veiled did their fair share of damage too. We were not the only victims. How many Veiled still lash out at humans without the mortals ever knowing why they were attacked? You know as well as I that some made it a sport for many years. Some still do. Besides'— he gives me a warm smile— 'while I have every faith in Esta, it takes more than one mortal girl to start a new war.'

I think I actually stop breathing when he looks at me. When I finally exhale, it comes out in a stutter, like my heart needs a good restart. Why does he have to be so attractive when he lectures people? Damn him and his reason. Damn me and my lack of the same.

The Mara and the Dreamcatcher go deathly still. I'm worried we and our good intentions ruined it.

But then the Mara looks up at the Dreamcatcher. 'If it is meant to be, it will be, no matter what we decide here today.

Even she can't change that.'

I get the feeling again that she doesn't mean me.

'No,' the Dreamcatcher says. 'But she will try.'

The Mara turns her blind eyes on me. 'And if it's meant to be, her actions won't truly matter. At most she might delay the inevitable or hurry it along a little.'

'Or they will, and she will throw us all into Chaos.'

The Mara shoots him another look that any human would understand as *shut the fuck up*. The Dreamcatcher gets the hint, too.

'We can make our own decisions, can't we?' The Mara looks at me again, and I'm beginning to think that she sees more than anyone with perfect eyesight could. 'You're a curious person, Esta Anderson.' She chuckles to herself like it's a private joke. The Dreamcatcher's neck snaps to the side and back again like he's in on it too.

'We will withdraw,' he says.

I want to fall to my knees in relief, but I do my best to stand strong.

'Can you tell us anything about who's after Esta?' Leverett asks.

The Mara studies me for a moment, then shakes her head. 'We have already done too much by going against her wishes. We cannot do more than that, but we can say this: She cannot interfere directly, and she is afraid for good reason. Be careful.'

I want to say that everything they've done to my dreams feels like plenty interference to me, but I bite my tongue again. What do I know? I've barely scratched the surface.

'I wonder how long you'll be able to uphold your quest for

peace,' the Dreamcatcher says.

The Mara tilts her head. 'We will be watching, Esta Anderson.'

They disappear in a slow puff of smoke, not that dissimilar to how Leverett turns to fog.

Bonnie lets out a massive sigh of relief. Lady strides around my legs and whines up at me.

'Is it over?' Bonnie asks.

I want to say *yes*, but I don't believe it. 'I think *this* fight is.'

Even so, I can't help feeling like I haven't seen anything yet. I thought the Dreamcatcher was after me, and I was wrong. Then I thought the Mara was after me, and that also turned out to be wrong. Someone else was behind all this, but who? Hopefully, my dreams are finally mine again, but I'm no closer to answers.

Bonnie glances around the room. 'Cocktail? To celebrate?'

Despite everything, I smile. There might be more to come, but we've earned a break.

I look between Leverett and Kate. 'Can we get you anything as a thank you?'

Bonnie wiggles her eyebrows at me as if to ask, *And what are you planning on serving him?* I blush and hope Leverett missed it.

I don't want to think about how this might have gone if I hadn't had their help. I'm okay. We're *all* okay. That's all that matters.

'I think you two deserve a moment to yourselves,' Kate says. 'I will leave you to recover, but Esta? I don't make empty promises. I said I would teach you, and I intend to do just that.'

Her words feel heavier than they sound. I swallow a lump in my throat. 'Understood.'

I'm excited at the prospect of learning more from Kate. She's already taught me so much that I can't help wondering how her next lessons will differ. If it means I get to ask her why the Mara called her Mother, I'm game for anything.

'I will excuse myself too,' Leverett says. I can't decide if I'm disappointed or relieved. 'Come by the bookshop when you're feeling up to it.'

'I will.'

He smiles at me, and I blush again. No, I'm definitely relieved. I need a moment to calm down after everything that happened. I'm fairly sure he's bad for my cardiac health right now. I may not be any less tense around him tomorrow, but at least I'll have had a good night's sleep, or I hope so, anyway. It'll be easier to think straight again tomorrow.

The moment the door closes, Bonnie and I burst into nervous giggles. The stress of the last days vanishes. I cannot wait to hug Mischief, but first I want to have normal day without fear of what tonight will bring.

So I hug Lady instead—she *was* the goodest girl for alerting Bonnie by barking up the stairs, telling us about the Mara—and then I pour us both some gin.

CHAPTER
EIGHTEEN

That night, I sleep better than ever. I want to explore every corner of my dreams, see everything I missed before, but I lie in the shade of my purple-leafed tree with Mischief and enjoy the normality. I tried calling Bonnie over, and I don't know if it's because we haven't had more of that tea or because the fear is missing now, but I can't find her again. We're confined to our own unconscious, and after all the nightmares, I don't mind it. We'll try again one day. Right now, the peace and quiet is perfection.

When I get up the next morning—I slept until just gone ten—Bonnie is outside and reading in the garden. I quickly get dressed, make myself and Lady a tea and Bonnie a coffee, and join her in the garden.

'Good morning, sleepy head,' she says when I sit next to her. 'How did you sleep?'

I stretch until my joints click. 'Wonderfully.' I put our drinks onto the low wall. 'Have a coffee. Read anything good?'

'Thank you.' She sips her drink. 'Kate loaned me a book about lucid dreaming techniques. We kicked butt yesterday.

It'd be cool to do it again.'

I nod and drink half of my tea. After the last few nights, I'm still tired even after my lie-in, but I also feel more awake than ever. The nightmares were terrifying, made all the more horrible by the Dreamcatcher's intention, but they've also shown me a whole new world. The Veiled are made up of fairies, playful demon children, and friendly vampires, but it's also made up of dream monsters and ancient beings that do not want to be found. I'm scared of what she—whoever *she* is—will send after me next, but I'm also excited.

I meant what I said to the Mara and the Dreamcatcher—I want to see it all. I won't turn away from any of it, and I won't endanger it. There are secrets out there that want to be protected, many of which are secret for good reason. My promise not to do the project was sincere, as was my promise to help. If there's anything I can do to defend this community, I'll do it. If I have to fight off hordes of people to keep them hidden, I will.

'We can try again whenever you're ready,' I say with a nod to the book.

We didn't do much the rest of the day—we didn't have the energy for much, so we just took Lady for a walk and saw everything with new eyes. I don't know what changed, but Bonnie sees them now, too. Kate said it could be because she entered my mind and touched on whatever the void lake did to me. I wonder if it's because she's now seen a vampire, the Mara, and the Dreamcatcher. How much proof do you need before your brain accepts what's right in front of you? Whatever did it, Bonnie sees everything I see. We don't stare.

We continue on our walk and talk about that fairy's wings or that werewolf's fur only once we're back home.

'What will you do?' Bonnie asks.

I shrug. 'I don't really know. Go back to Leverett's shop for more books?'

'You should tell him how you feel.'

I snort into my cup. 'I don't think so.'

'What if he feels the same way? Isn't it better to know than to wonder and regret?'

I playfully punch her arm. 'When did you get so wise? And does this mean you'll tell your diving instructor?'

She blushes and giggles. 'I don't know what you mean.'

'Uh-huh. So you're not into her?'

Bonnie smirks. 'I didn't say that. We actually have a date tomorrow.'

I smile. 'That's great. I hope it goes well.' I feel terrible that we've barely talked about this lady. It's not fair that I've hogged all the attention lately. 'When can I meet her?'

Bonnie blushes deeper. 'When you tell Leverett you lurve him.'

My laugh comes out as a strange, nervous, strangled sound. 'Again, I don't think so.'

Painful as it is, it feels good to talk about something so normal as our love lives, even if mine involves the unreturned affection of a vampire.

'So, if not that, what will you do?' Bonnie asks. 'Are you really not sure?'

I lean back. 'I want to help, but I don't know how if I can't interact with them.'

'We'll figure it out,' Bonnie says. 'Step by step, hm?'

'We?' I ask with a smile.

'I told you, we were awesome in your dream. Like a Veiled defence force.'

I laugh again, more normal this time. 'We're awesome outside my dream, too. It'll be like that time we were five and decided to protect all the cats in our street.'

Only, the Veiled are neither defenceless nor made up of tiny animals.

She giggles. 'Just with more monsters.'

I roll my eyes. 'Please, the assholes who are mean to cats are the real monsters.' I meant it as a joke, but I also mean every word.

We have a lazy day watching *Charmed* repeats on TV. Despite my lie-in, I struggle to stay awake until my usual bedtime and excuse myself early. It's nice to not be scared of my dreams again. Order has been restored, at least in my unconscious.

Mischief greets me by strolling around my feet. 'What shall we do tonight?'

I smile into the distance.

'Show me something new.'

Esta's ability to become conscious in her dreams isn't fiction. Lucid dreaming is a skill like any other and can be learned! If Esta and I have made you curious, here's a quick guide to get started:

- **You can start by keeping a dream diary.** The simple act of writing down your dreams will help you remember them, even if you don't actually remember anything. On those days, just write 'I don't remember any dreams from last night.'

- Your recall will improve faster than you think. I recommend keeping to symbolism rather than every little detail, or it can become very time-consuming. The longest I've needed to write down every detail of one dream was over an hour!

- **Performing reality checks throughout the day is a good way to become aware in your dreams.** Do it often enough and you'll automatically start checking in your dreams, too!

- While you're awake, look at something permanent or slow-changing. I prefer to count the fingers on my hands, but in your dreams you may find seeing ten fingers in rainbow colours on each hand scary, so proceed with care—you don't want to wake yourself up from the shock!

- You could also check the time (look at a watch or a clock, look away for two seconds, then look at the time again). While you're awake, time doesn't change that fast, but in your dream, the clock face may show a different time or change entirely.

- **Two popular techniques are called WILD (wake induced lucid dream) and MILD (mnemonic induced lucid dream).** Personally, I like to combine the two!

- For WILD, you can set an alarm for roughly four hours after you go to sleep (or count on your bladder to wake you, like me). Get up for a little bit, then go back to bed.

- (Please note that I consider four hours to be rough guidance rather than a rule. I find this works best for me at the weekends when I don't need to get up early. I don't set an alarm, I just wake up naturally, walk around a little, then go back to bed.)

- For MILD, all you need to do is remember the last dream you had as you fall back asleep. Make it as detailed as you can. Chances are good you'll wake up in your next dream!

- In my experience, a combination of all of the above works best.

Don't be discouraged if it takes a while. You're learning a new skill, and it's not something you can practice for hours at a time. Be patient with yourself, and you will get there.

If you'd like further guidance or to discuss other techniques, feel free to reach out on my social media accounts. The links are in the back of this book.

The Mara

It might seem strange that I've decided to write a series including as much mythology and folklore as I possibly can, and then open with a creature I've invented. If you're as interested in mythology as I am, you've likely come across the Mara before, but the Dreamcatcher?

He's one of mine.

Even so, I wanted to provide a little background for those of you wanting to know more about his friend and colleague, the Mara.

Depending on which country you look at, you might know the Mara as Mora, Mare, or Moroi, to name a few variations. It's thought that the word *nightmare* is related to the Mara.

The first mention of her in literature is in the Norse Ynglinga saga from the thirteenth century, but she is likely far older than that. It's possible that she was an early explanation for sleep paralysis.

Usually, the Mara is considered a goblin or an evil spirit who sits/rides on the sleeper's chest to bring forth nightmares. In Norwegian and Danish, the words for nightmare translate to "mare-ride".

I don't believe that anyone or anything is fully good or evil, though—rather we're all different shades of grey—so the Mara's place in Esta's story isn't really an evil one either. We're all complex creatures, Maras and Dreamcatchers included.

Thank you so much for reading *A Dream of Death and Magic*. This book means a lot to me, and your support does too. I hope you've had as much fun with Esta as I did! I'm really looking forward to writing the sequels. Hopefully, you're looking forward to reading them.

If you have two minutes, I'd be grateful a review. This helps readers find their next favourite book, so your review or even just a rating makes a big difference. It doesn't need to be long, either! One sentence (or again, just a rating) is plenty.

Thank you.

Like freebies?

Join my mailing list and receive my novella *Shadow in Ar'Sanciond* and the short story *Pashros Kai Zo* (which isn't available anywhere else!) for free. You'll also hear about upcoming releases, early cover reveals, exclusive giveaways, excerpts, and all other announcements. Join at: subscribepage.com/sarinasbooks

If you'd like to hang out with me in an informal setting and get early peeks at new covers and maps, join my Facebook Reader Group 'Sarina's Sparrows': facebook.com/groups/sarinassparrows

Let's Connect

sarinalanger.com
goodreads.com/sarinalangerwriter
twitter.com/sarina_langer
patreon.com/sarinalanger

Acknowledgments

This is the 9th book I've published and the 10th book I've written. Usually, it's time to write the acknowledgments and I'm tired. Usually, something or other has complicated the writing process or maybe the publishing itself. I'll still love the characters, of course, but I'll also be ready to look at a different world, characters, etc.

With *A Dream of Death and Magic*, this isn't the case. I can't wait to bring you more books in this series. Honestly! This book is really rather personal to me. It means a lot, and I'm so excited that I've currently got another 9 (and at least one novella – one is already written because I got carried away) planned. There's so much to explore, and I can't wait to dive in deeper. This book has been a joy from start to finish, and I hope that you felt some of that love as you read it.

My first shout-out goes to my very first critique partners, who read an early version of this story a couple of years or so ago. I think we all learned from this experience that I cannot pantse a book and must never do it again. Thank you for sticking with it and already loving Esta back then, when her first journey was so rough in every respect. Thank you to Beverley Lee, Rhianne Roynon, Dana Fraedrich, Faith Rivens, and Jessica Reis.

Thank you to my second set of critique partners, who read an early draft of this story after I started over from scratch. I had my plotter hat on again for this round, and I believe we can all agree that I work much better this way. Thank you to Jules Appleton, Tris Prewitt, and Tasha Rook. I very much wrote this with you in mind.

This was my first time working with an alpha reader. Thank you to my Bonnie, Miriam Kurtoglu, for reading the first draft of Esta's journey and already loving her then (not that *first* first draft though; not the version I pantsed a few years ago). I might have been offended if you hadn't. (kidding) (mostly)

Thank you to Rae Oestreich for being a stellar editor and helping me draw even more magic out of this book. Thank you also for letting me message you any time to discuss a beta comment or discuss an idea or potential change. You always know just how to put my mind at ease and say just the right thing, and I'm eternally grateful to you.

Thank you to Becky at Platform House Publishing for creating the beautiful interior.

Thank you to Diablerie GraphicArts for creating this stunning new cover and for putting so much love and time into it. I'm thrilled that you love these books as much as I do <3

Thank you to my beta readers Dana Fraedrich, TaniaRina Perry, and Keina Darya for helping me further strengthen this book. And a special note to Dana: you've no idea how much your feedback made me smile and laugh. I even included your fluffy floor shark's popcorn habits as an Easter Egg only you will notice.

Thank you to Esta, Bonnie, Leverett, and Kate for being so incredibly chatty and forthcoming. Because of you, this was a pleasure to write and even edit. Here's to another 9 books and some short stories and novellas together.

A special thank you goes to my Patreon Sparrows and my Facebook Reader Group. I'm grateful for how involved you've been in this story, helping me choose a title, helping me choose quotes, helping me name the dog, being the first to see the cover (in its very early stages, in Patreon's case!), etc. You've made an already enjoyable WIP even more enjoyable!

Thank *you* for reading this book. I hope you love it as much as I do. There's a lot more coming towards Esta – this was only the beginning in more ways than one. Thank you also if you take the time to rate or even review. It really means a lot. Seeing everyone's excitement and love for this book makes my day. Until next time, dear Sparrows.

About the Author

Sarina is an epic/dark fantasy author and freelance editor from the south of England, where she lives with her partner and her daughter (read: her cat).

She is as obsessed with books and stationery now as she was as a child, when she drowned her box of colour pencils in water so they wouldn't die and scribbled her first stories on corridor walls.

('A first sign of things to come', according to her mother. 'Normal toddler behaviour', according to Sarina.)

In her free time, she has a weakness for books, pretty words, and plays video games.

She believes that the best books are those where every ray of light casts a shadow.